WHAT PEOPLE ARE SAYING ABOUT THE CANAAN CREED

"This is a provocative page-turner telling its story from a perspective not often found in modern fiction. This book's well-drawn characters and suspenseful plot ensures that it cannot be pigeonholed by political or social philosophy. However, Americans need to heed the moral of the story, lest we find ourselves in an untenable situation. I really enjoyed the book and I'm already looking forward to the next one from L.P. Hoffman!"
— Craig Manson, Distinguished Professor and Lecturer, University of the Pacific McGeorge School of Law, and Former Assistant Secretary of the Interior

"L.P. Hoffman knows the West intimately and evokes issues with sure-footed familiarity."
— C.J. Box, Author of THREE WEEKS TO SAY GOODBYE

"The Canaan Creed weaves suspense, mystery and the dark side of environmental fanaticism together to create a page-turning story that keeps the reader hooked until the very end. The story connects the reader with the awe-inspiring beauty of nature, while exposing how many environmental zealots have turned the experience into a nature-worshipping religion, and others exploit the movement for personal profit and power. While the book is far from being anti-environment, it clearly defines how false environmental scare stories are often created or exaggerated to advance an anti-human agenda which is penetrating our public schools and federal agencies. In the process, people's lives are inevitably harmed and all too often destroyed."
— Michael S. Coffman, Ph.D., President of Environmental Perspectives, Inc.

The CANAAN CREED

The CANAAN CREED

A NOVEL BY
L. P. HOFFMAN

WWW.HOPESPRINGSMEDIA.COM

THE CANAAN CREED
BY L.P. HOFFMAN

www.thecanaancreed.com

Published by Hope Springs Media
www.hopespringsmedia.com
P.O. Box 11, Prospect, Virginia 23960-0011
Toll-Free (866) 964-2031 Fax: (434) 574-2030

International Standard Book Number:
978-1-935375-00-5

Printed in the United States of America

This book is a work of fiction.
Any similarities to actual people or places are unintentional.

Cover design by Hope Springs Media and Exodus Design

This book is dedicated to:
God~Creator of the heavens and the earth,
Paul, my beloved, for standing beside me at the helm,
even during rough and rocky waters,
Desiree, my loving daughter, and
Fritz, who always believed.

Special thanks to Wendy Prevost whose heaven~sent
encouragement kept me afloat on the days when my
heart felt swamped.

My gratitude also goes to Kathy Ide and Frances
Hazelwood, my gifted editors, for their
challenging insights.

*Tis good
when the man loves the land.
Tis good when he falls for his creed,
But woe to the hate that is fanned
By folly begotten of greed.*

Edgar Wallace, 1875

PROLOGUE

Canaan Island, Maine
Saturday, June 3

Malcolm O'Neil did not want to believe the thoughts that had driven him to climb the cliffy shoreline of Canaan Island at dawn. But instinct fueled his trek. There was no time to waste. The acid taste of fear coated his tongue as he picked his way along a jagged outcropping. He slipped, nearly tumbling into the cold waters, but regained his balance and continued around the narrow point.

On the other side of the point, a small sandy cove came into view. Malcolm hurried along a short inlet to a hidden beach. There, he scrambled up a stair-step ledge of rocks that led to a cleft carved by centuries of wind. With agile fingers, he probed the upper edge of the polished granite as if it were a secret message written in Braille.

Sweat dripped from damp strands of Malcolm's gray hair and stung his eyes. Finally, he located the narrow crevice. It was just as he had remembered—dry and safely elevated from the tide.

At his back, the rhythmic sound of the Atlantic's waves whooshed closer. The morning sun yawned across the ocean with a breathy golden mist, casting an eerie light upon the cliff.

Malcolm removed a plastic envelope from his belt, rolled it tight, and wedged it deep within the little cavern. "It's done," he said, and hurried from the sheltered cove to beat the tidal surge.

He lingered on the rocky point. His thoughts turned to Anna. Sorrow filled his heart as he envisioned his daughter standing on that very beach, sun kissed and full of life. "God help her," Malcolm prayed as he turned away. Behind him, the tide rolled in to guard his secret, swallowing all traces of his footsteps in the foamy mire.

CHAPTER 1

Oh East is East, and West is West,
and never the twain shall meet,
Till earth and sky stand presently at
God's great judgment seat;
Rudyard Kipling

Wyoming
Saturday, June 3

As Anna O'Neil threw open one of the double doors of the Cedar Ridge community center, the moist, musky smell of sweat assaulted her—remnants of Wednesday's aerobics class. The moderate-sized building served as the town gymnasium, dance hall, and theater, however, on this particular evening, it was the epicenter of a controversy.

"All for the greater good," the young biologist said under her breath as she nudged past a cluster of locals. "Let the fireworks begin." The auditorium was crowded and unbearably stuffy on such a warm summer night.

Anna glanced around for a place to sit and wished she'd come earlier. Her eye caught sight of some portable stairs in the rear of the room. A group of high school students had claimed the spot, but they gladly made room for Anna, whom they treated as a folk hero. She took a seat on the top step and engaged the youth on either side of her in a spattering of superficial conversation.

Tension electrified the atmosphere. Lively discussion undulated with anxious, sometimes angry words.

When a man in a uniform with a government emblem stepped to the microphone at the front of the room, all eyes fixed on him. He adjusted his bolo tie, flipped open a notebook, and cleared his throat. The field office rep switched on the projector. "Will everyone please take a seat so we can get started?" He pushed his wire-frame glasses up on his nose, fiddled with the remote control, and waited for the people to settle down.

"We've got quite a turnout tonight." He smiled, but few smiled back. "As regional director for the US Fish and Wildlife Service, I am here to gather public comments concerning our draft proposal for the reintroduction and management of gray wolves. Please direct your questions and comments to me and keep them short." The man slid a pen from his shirt pocket and, with the aid of colored maps, explained five alternative proposals. He droned on and on about existing policy, his voice flat and monotone.

The crowd, on the verge of stupor, stirred when the

director switched off the overhead. The room grew quiet, except for a baby fussing in the back.

"Are there any comments?" The director looked across the pool of faces.

"I got a question." A heavy-set woman wearing a blue bandana stood. "The first two options talk about keeping the wolves in Yellowstone. Does that mean you're gonna fence the national park?"

The regional director picked at his finger. "That is really not feasible."

"Then why'd ya put those alternatives in there?" someone yelled.

"I must ask for raised hands so everything can be done in an orderly fashion." Avoiding the last question, the director called on a cadaverous-looking man holding a pen and paper.

"I understand that a wildlife group has offered to pay for any livestock killed by a wolf until the wolves' legal status changes in Wyoming. Could you please clarify when that will be?" The man's pen hovered above the notepad.

"Not until the gray wolf is no longer listed as an endangered species." He pointed to another audience member. "The man in the red plaid shirt."

"What can we do about wolves killing our livestock?"

The regional director's face flushed. "If you witness a wolf in the process of killing an animal, you may shoot," he said cautiously.

"That's crazy, mister," the man said. "How am I supposed to watch more than four hundred head of cattle spread out over five thousand acres of leased range land?"

"Ship all the wolves to Washington, DC!" an angry man bellowed.

The director's face went rigid. "Statements like that aren't going to get us very far." He searched the room and pointed to Anna, whose hand was in the air. "The young woman in the tank top and khaki shorts."

All faces turned to Anna O'Neil as she sprang from her seat and hurried to the front of the room. She stopped at the microphone, looked over the tumultuous crowd, and ran her fingers through short, sun-bleached hair. "As a wildlife biologist, I have studied this issue. The reintroduction of the gray wolf to Yellowstone would not only be beneficial to the ecosystem, but these majestic animals would also support other wildlife. Bald eagles and bears feed on the carcasses they leave behind. Overpopulated herds of ungulates, especially elk, would be thinned making room for small plant-eating animals."

From the back of the room a horse-faced woman yelled, "Yeah, you talking about rats?"

Anna leveled her gaze on the woman who seemed to shrink in her seat. "Small rodents and beavers to name a few." She paused to collect her thoughts. "I appeal to you from my heart tonight." Anna cleared her throat and did her best to ignore the cynical rustling among the townspeople. "Nature is in trouble and she needs our cooperation. Each of us should give back a portion of what we've taken from this planet. Since the ranchers appear to be ones most threatened by the concept of biodiversity addressed by the reintroduction of the gray wolf, I direct my appeal mainly to them."

The crowd started buzzing, gnashing angry words her way. Anna stubbornly pressed on. "Historically, wolves were a token of the West. This changed in the early 1900's with the implementation of predator programs. The wolves, already struggling from man-induced game shortages, faced extinction."

"I knew it!" A man in an orange hunter's vest shot to his feet and pointed a gnarled finger at Anna. "Pretty soon the government won't even allow us to hunt. Next thing we know, people like you will be taking away our guns!"

Anna fought to remain calm. "Wolves are part of a delicately balanced ecosystem, and as such, they are a natural tool for sound game management."

The crowd grew louder.

"We have a chance to redeem the wrongs of our past," Anna called out, "In order to do this, we must look past our own interests and bring the gray wolf home to Yellowstone!"

Hostile rumblings flattened cheers and hoots raised from the young people sitting on the bleachers.

An old rancher rose to his feet and pushed a bent

straw hat back on his forehead. He raised his hand and motioned to the townspeople. A hush fell over the group. "Young lady, all your high talk about ecosystems doesn't mean much if those mangy canines are running my herd all over the range," he said scratching his leathered chin. "Think about that next time you sit down for a New York steak." Laughter rippled through the room.

Anna's face felt flushed and she hoped it didn't show. "I am a vegetarian." With head held high, she stepped from the podium and trailed through the crowd amidst a chorus of boos and hisses.

"Ladies and gentlemen," the director said with raised voice, "everyone here has a right to express his or her opinion without any outbursts. Please, show some respect."

"Awesome!" A high school student gave Anna a thumbs-up as she returned to the bleachers where her fellow environmentalists had congregated. They resembled a band of rag-tag mountaineers in their wrinkled cotton shorts, tattered wool sweaters, and Birkenstocks. Though mostly young, they had their share of white-haired zealots, like Addison Lee, founder and president of the Pristine Valley Nature Coalition.

Addison stood at the end of her row, leaning his thin body casually against the wall. His eyes met Anna's as she approached, and he extended a smooth white hand to her. "You stood strong, my dear." Addison bent close to her ear and lowered his voice, "although I'm afraid many of the locals are beyond reason." He laid his hand on Anna's shoulder. "I'd like to have a word with you," Addison said, steering her toward the entryway.

They stopped just beyond the gymnasium doors. "What's going on?" Anna asked.

"I have some news that I hope will please you." He paused as if to savor the moment. "You have been selected to represent our efforts in Wyoming at the upcoming summit in Geneva, Switzerland."

Anna laughed, but Addison's face was serious. "Me?" She touched her chest.

He slipped an itinerary from his pocket and handed it to her. "I took the liberty of arranging for your travel and accommodations. All you need to do is pack." A toying half smile spread across Addison's face. "There's just one little detail. You should have a speech prepared. It need not be anything long or pretentious. Some of the things you said tonight will do just fine."

Anna took a deep breath, trying to take it all in. "A speech?" She repeated his words as if that would help them sink in. "But why?"

Addison broke into a full smile. "My dear, you have been nominated to receive this year's Gaia award."

Anna nearly staggered backward at the news. Her head was awhirl with thoughts, yet none settled long enough to put into words. Some of the most influential people in the world would attend the prestigious nature summit: heads of state, ambassadors, financial moguls, and celebrities. Anna thought of her father and imagined him doing a cartwheel on the beach when he heard the news. "You're sure they want me?"

"The international community is very interested in what goes on in Yellowstone National Park." Addison's thin lips pressed into a tight smile. "And you, my dear, have a true passion for the cause."

Anna's heart pounded as she envisioned the future. The course was set before her. What could possibly go wrong?

CHAPTER 2

Fear oftentimes restraineth words,
but makes not thought to cease;
And he speaks best that hath the skill
when for to hold his peace.
Thomas Vaux

Wyoming
Thursday, June 8

At the Broken Arrow Dude Ranch, Reuben Fischer grabbed his duffle bag and blew through the screen door of the main lodge without looking back. His wife raced after him, snapping at his ears like a pit bull. "I want to know what you were doing in Cedar Ridge this morning!"

"Dance lessons—what do you think?" he quipped without turning back. "I was picking up supplies."

"I think you were having coffee!" she challenged.

Reuben halted and faced his wife.

The abruptness of his movement temporarily derailed Cassandra, but she quickly recovered. "I knew it!

You sat around drinking coffee and leaving all the work for me!" She parked her hands on bony hips and set her chin defiantly. "Don't you think I have better things to do than pick up your slack? I made a mistake when I married you. I should have finished my degree in journalism. Now I'm stuck on this mountain with a husband who won't even talk to me!"

Words roiled behind Reuben's tongue but he held them in. He turned toward the corrals, hoping none of the dude ranch's guests were in earshot of his wife's tantrum.

"That's right, just skip out on your responsibilities," Cassandra shrieked. "Go ahead. Ride up the mountain like my dad!"

Reuben lengthened his stride but his wife closed the gap.

"Just like always," she said. "Running away!"

"It's called business, Cassandra. We have a fishing camp to set up."

Cassandra threw her head back and shrieked. "Three days early?"

"I'd ride my horse all the way to Florida if it would make things peaceful around here." Reuben opened the corral gate.

Cassandra turned on her heals and stomped back to the lodge, leaving a few choice words hanging in the air.

The hired wrangler had Reuben's bay-colored horse saddled and ready to ride. "Thought ya could use a head start."

"Thanks, Kip." Rueben rubbed a tension knot from his neck. "How long ago did Duke ride up the trail?"

"'Bout fifteen, maybe twenty minutes ago," the wrangler said, untying the halter rope. He fired a tobacco missile through the gap in his teeth. "I filled some panniers. Got yer mule string lined out, too."

The front door of the lodge slammed hard behind Cassandra, and a quiet settled over the ranch. It reminded Reuben of the ominous calm in the Vietnam jungle—just before the enemy exploded on the scene. There was no telling when Cassandra would strike again.

A sense of loss bordering on grief plagued Reuben as he recalled the early years of their marriage. How had it come to this?

Reuben mounted up, tipped his hat to the wrangler, and reined his horse. He cast a heavy glance toward home. On the porch, his fourteen-year-old son stood watching. Cordell raised his hand and waved at his father. Reuben felt a rush of guilt as he waved back. One of these days, he'd take the boy along, but at the moment, the thought of another confrontation with his wife was more than Reuben could bear.

With pack string in tow, he urged his horse into a trot. The mountain lay straight ahead, and to Reuben, that meant distance . . . blessed distance.

A half hour later, he caught up with his father-in-law, just below the lower switchbacks.

Duke shifted his saddle. "Didn't think you'd be far

behind me." The old rancher removed his hat, contemplated its shape, then cocked an eye toward Reuben. "Someone once said that a good hat gets better as it gets older. Just like a good cowboy." Duke ran a hand over a thinning scalp and coaxed his horse back onto the trail where he whittled away the hours spouting cowboy wisdom.

The two men stopped at their usual lunch spot: a small clearing on the shady side of the mountain where tree breaks framed a breathtaking view of a rugged mountain peak. At a creek that trickled through the meadow, Reuben hopped off his horse and knelt to drink his fill of the icy snowmelt.

Duke swung from his saddle, secured the pack string, and retrieved a couple of small brown sacks from the saddlebags. He ambled on his old bowed legs to a log, where he carefully lowered his arthritic frame.

Reuben caught the lunch sack that his father-in-law tossed his way. He settled down by a fallen tree to eat his sandwich. Except for the rustle of leaves and the chatter of a squirrel that jumped from branch to branch over their heads, the mountain was still.

Duke broke the silence. "I'm sorry," he said, brushing crumbs of bread from his rough hands.

"About what?" Reuben asked.

"Will Rodgers once said, 'There are two theories to arguing with a woman. Neither one works.'" The older man leaned back and stretched out his legs. "I'll probably never win the Father of the Year award. After her mama died, I spoiled Cassandra. I realize that now." Duke sucked air through his teeth. "Good judgment comes from experience—unfortunately, a lot of that comes from bad judgment."

Reuben said nothing, though he thought of plenty to say. *Maybe I could have done more to support her dreams.*

Duke leaned back to use the log as a pillow. "Well, I believe I'm gonna check my eyelids for pinholes." He set the cowboy hat over his face.

In the valley, an eagle circled effortlessly and turned toward Jagged Peak. Reuben watched until the magnificent bird flew out of sight. There was no place on God's earth he would rather be than here. In the mountains, everything down below seemed so small.

The sound of Duke's snoring rumbled and hissed like an old air compressor. A gentle breeze danced through the trees, playing a mosaic light show across the forest bed. Reuben felt himself getting drowsy, leaned back on a mound of earth to rest, and lapsed into a dream-haunted sleep.

Each step was painful, but he tried not to think about it. Reuben had seen jungle rot before and it was not a pretty sight. He trudged on through the shin-deep rice paddies. Reuben and the soldiers didn't know where they were going . . . only that there was no turning back.

He looked around at the handful of men in his

company. The soldiers were silent and bone-weary. Their eyes were raw with unspoken despair. Suddenly, like rhythmic music, the sound of choppers arose just beyond the horizon.

Hope soared among the troops. They jumped and shouted in jubilant praise. They had not been forgotten! They had not been left to die!

Reuben watched in surreal disbelief as the choppers banked sharply to the left and flew away. "No!" he called. The sounds of chaos erupted from the foliage nearby and a burning pain grazed his head. The last thing Reuben remembered before he dropped to his knees was the look of horror on the faces of his companions.

Reuben jolted from the nightmare as if he had been falling. His blood was pumping hard. He took a few deep breaths to calm himself. A rhythm met his ear. Was it the sound of a chopper?

He launched to his feet, hurried to the edge of the meadow, and tilted his head to listen. "Is this real?" he whispered, wondering if he was going crazy. The *foom-foom-foom* of the blades grew louder. A helicopter surfaced over the sunlit ridge and descended into a nearby clearing. Reuben scrambled down a small embankment to get a closer look. He carefully approached a thick stand of beetle-killed pines and crouched low to see what was going on.

The chopper touched down on the far side of the meadow. Its blades wound down to an idle.

Suddenly a bull moose thrashed wildly through the bramble, heading his way. Reuben scrambled to his feet and took cover behind one of bigger trees. He watched the large, cantankerous animal disappear into the thick timber.

"Hey!"

Reuben shot a look over his shoulder and saw his father-in-law, hurrying down the embankment.

"What the heck is going on over there?" Duke hollered.

Reuben lifted his finger to his mouth and pointed across the meadow. Together they watched two men unload large crates from the helicopter. A third man stood guard, sweeping the countryside with a pair of binoculars.

A prickly feeling stirred inside Reuben. "Get back."

From the shadows, Duke raised his voice. "Do you see what they're taking out of those boxes?"

Reuben had seen enough to know these men were up to no good. He fixed his eyes on the man with the field glasses who was talking to another man nearest the craft's cockpit. His companion nodded, leaned inside the helicopter's door, drew out an assault rifle, and pointed it toward the cowboys.

Reuben's legs felt like lead. "Run, Duke," he screamed. Primal fear flooded his senses.

The sound of gunfire reverberated through the mountains. Reuben dove for the ground as Duke raced to where he had tied his horse and quickly mounted up.

In the meadow, the chopper lifted off.

"Come on," the old man called over the whir of blades as the chopper appeared overhead. Duke's horse reared up. He hung on as Ol' Blue spun around.

Reuben watched helplessly as his father-in-law's mules erupted in a frenzied panic, catching him in the pack string's loops. Duke grimaced as the rope burned across his side. Mercifully, the tattered hemp snapped and the horse bolted off into the thicket, his rider holding on for dear life.

The chopper sank lower, staying just above the tree line. Swirling blades blew dry pine needles through the air and they rained onto the forest bed. A man leaned out of the aircraft, gun in hand.

Reuben ran as the sound of another rifle report rang in his ears and echoed through the mountains.

CHAPTER 3

Credula vitam Spes fovet, ac melius cras fore simper ait
—Credulous hope is kind to our life, and ever tells us
that tomorrow will be better than today
Latin-Tibullus

Wyoming
Friday, June 9

Grace Fischer stepped outside her Wyoming mountain cabin and breathed in a lung full of clean air. To her the scent of pine was always sweetest in the dawning hours. She lifted her eyes to the jagged peaks, their outline illuminated by the waking sun. Grace counted her blessings, as she did every morning. *God's country*, she thought, grateful to live in such a beautiful spot.

Near the edge of the creek, a mule deer jumped, flicked her tail to warn her twin fawns, and bolted through the meadow. Something had her spooked.

Grace's gaze shifted to the thirty-two stone steps that led from her cabin to the Fischer Creek Café and Gas

Station. Grace began her slow ascent. A breeze kicked up, sending her loose cotton dress flapping around her plump body like an unpegged tent. Midway up, she paused for a breather. For almost half a century, Grace had climbed these steps, ever since she first arrived in the Pristine Valley as a young bride. That was back when the Fischer name still carried some weight around these parts—too many years ago to count.

Grace pressed on, doing a mental check of her morning chores: Start the coffee, bake the biscuits, and make another batch of cookie dough.

Just short of the Fischer Creek Café and Gas Station, she tilted her head to the sound of a motor fading down the road. "Probably a pilgrim," she said to herself. They arrived earlier every year it seemed.

Near the cafe's back kitchen door, Grace lingered to inspect the petunias she had planted yesterday beside the wall. The cold night air had taken its toll. She touched a wilted petal and shook her head. "A little sunshine will cure what ails you."

Grace lifted the watch pendant that hung from her neck. It was time to get busy. She stooped to retrieve the key from its hiding place in the old pot-bellied stove beside the back door, but she found no key.

Strange. Grace was sure it had been there when she'd locked up last night. She checked again, did a quick visual sweep of the grounds, then hurried back down the stone steps toward the old cabin she shared with her husband.

In the tiny kitchen, Grace found Milo seated at a drop-leaf table amid sections of newspaper. "Did you see this article?" he said without looking up. "You know that little wolf biologist gal, the one who's been stirring things up around here?" He pointed to her picture.

"Anna O'Neil," Grace said, still wheezing after her trek up and down all those steps.

"She's been nominated for some kind of award in Switzerland," Milo scowled. "Can you believe it?"

"That's nice." Grace did her best to ignore her husband's sharp look.

"Nice?" Milo's brow rose.

"Honey, I can't find the key to the café. I need your spare."

Her husband folded his newspaper and tossed it on the cluttered table, knocking over some knickknacks. "When are you gonna get rid of all this junk?" Milo glared at the collection of salt-and-pepper shakers. Grudgingly, he shoved his hand into the back hip pocket of his Carhart overalls and retrieved a crowded key chain, that he tossed to his wife.

"Do you remember which one is the back door key?" Grace asked, examining each one.

Milo's face wrinkled with a sour expression. "For crying out loud, woman." He snatched back the keys. "Do I have to do everything around here?" The elderly man pushed his wiry frame from the chair and stomped out the door with a grunt.

The morning light reflected on Milo's shiny bald head as he marched up the steps. By the time Grace caught up, he was muttering to himself.

One of the keys slid into the lock and Milo pushed the door open. "There, now, that wasn't so hard, was it?" He flashed crooked teeth in a sheepish smile, gave his wife's shoulder a playful squeeze and escorted her inside.

Grace had always been able to see right through her husband's gruff exterior. Milo was like a high-strung child who viewed the world as a scary place and reacted with false bravado.

He stopped just inside the kitchen. Milo's eyes shifted back and forth. "Do you smell smoke?" He sniffed the air.

Grace hurried through the commercial kitchen. "Nothing here," she called. "I think it's coming from the dining room!"

Her heart thumped with panic as she pushed open the swinging doors. Grace's gaze swept over the breakfast counter and across a sea of gingham checked tablecloths. Her eyes froze on a portable radiator, glowing orange. Above it, a smoldering curtain exploded in flames. A startled scream escaped from Grace's lips.

Milo blew past her with a fire extinguisher, doused the flame, and yanked the blackened curtains from the wall. Shaking, he turned to Grace. "What the heck is wrong with you, woman?" Flushed with anger, he jerked the heater's plug from the wall. "You could have wiped us out!"

"I didn't do this," Grace said. Her voice was calm but insistent. "I didn't put the heater there."

"Well, you don't think I did it, do you?"

"Good heavens no, but ... " Grace's mind wandered as she inspected the damage to the red-and-blue flower-print curtains and tried to remember their age— fifteen, maybe twenty years old. New ones were definitely in order, she decided.

Through the window, a movement caught Grace's eye. Across the road from the café, a solitary young man stood, his backpack resting on the ground beside him. He was a Native American, she noted, observing his dark braided hair. Grace had never seen him before, but he seemed to be watching the café "Probably just waiting for us to open," she told herself, and turned back to the task at hand. "Oh, gracious, we need to air this place out!"

"I'll open the windows," Milo said. "You take care of this mess."

When Grace looked back through the window, the stranger was gone.

She slipped into the utility closet to retrieve a mop and bucket. Grace returned to find Milo tapping on the windowpane to loosen old paint. With a heave, he opened the window. Fresh air poured into the café.

"First the missing key, and now this," Milo said. "Either you're getting forgetful or someone was trying to burn us down."

"I am certainly not becoming forgetful," she said.

"And for heavens sake, who would want to set fire to the café?" Grace filled the bucket with water and swirled the mop over the ashes.

Before long, they fell into their usual routines. Grace loaded the coffee makers, put flames on under the pot of gravy, and slid a tray of biscuits into the oven.

Milo disappeared into the small convenience store on the far side of the building. "I'm going to activate the gas pumps," he called.

"Might as well do a quick inventory of the shelves," Grace said. "We're running low on snacks and soda pop."

Within the hour, the regulars began to arrive to occupy their favorite spots at the old knotty-pine counter and Milo returned to play host. He entertained the patrons with a recap of the morning's excitement. "If it wasn't for my quick thinking, this whole place would be a pile of cinders."

"Traveler's special," Grace said, placing a generous plate of ham and eggs on the order window.

"Morning, Gracie," one of the regulars called. "I hear you're married to a hero."

"Well, somebody had to marry him," she said, retreating into the kitchen.

"Biscuits and gravy and two more specials," Milo yelled as he clipped the orders to the wheel.

The morning sped by in a flurry of steam and grease. By 11:00 AM, Grace was grateful for a lull.

Turning to wipe her hands on her apron, she jumped at the sight of a large man standing in the doorway. "Dillon! Goodness, you gave me a start."

"Hi, Ma." He kissed his mother on the cheek, then followed her to the stove.

Grace reached for the freshly brewed pot of coffee and poured her son a cup.

Though Dillon was the younger of her two grown boys, he was by far the biggest, in both bulk and height. Milo used to joke that the stork made the wrong delivery, but no one could deny that Dillon was a Fischer in temperament—just like his dad.

"Are you hungry?" she asked.

Dillon didn't answer. He pulled a square of paper from his plaid shirt pocket. "They closed access to Slough Creek Pass. You can't even get past the old mill road. They put up a metal gate." Dillon unfolded the paper, but in a fit of anger crushed it in his hand. "That's what I think of these new regulations."

Grace reached out for her son, but he paced out of her reach. "Slough Creek Pass has been a public access for as long as I can remember. Why would anyone put up a gate?"

Dillon scowled. "I'd like to know the answer to that question too. I have a firewood contract with the forest service and they're not holding up their end."

Dillon lurched to a stop by the old black wall phone and thumbed through the directory that hung next to it. "You'd think I would know the number by now." He punched the buttons. "I want to talk to someone about the closure of the Slough Creek access."

His mother tried not to eavesdrop, but Dillon's terse words told all.

"I've got a lumber quota to meet. How am I supposed to fill my obligations when you pull this kind of . . .?"

Grace took a sip of coffee, noting worry lines on her son's face. She whispered a quiet prayer as Dillon slammed the receiver down.

Red faced, he looked at his mother. "They've ordered an environmental impact statement. Can you believe it? I asked 'em why and they said, 'to minimize future damage to the region.'" Dillon stripped his cap from his head and ran his hand through a disheveled head of hair. "I don't know what damage they're talking about. I'm the only one who logs up there, and I've always gone out of my way to be responsible."

"Heavens, yes. Everyone knows you only cut down the beetle-killed pine for firewood, nothing green." Grace wished her words would calm her son, but Dillon was too much like his father.

He paced the room with a wild, jerky stride. "And whenever I get a contract for building logs, I only do thinning cuts. The growth up there is probably healthier now than it was twenty years ago. I guess that's not good enough!"

Grace saw fear in her youngest son's eyes and longed to comfort him—to help him try to make sense of things. Her stomach churned. Was Slough Creek a portent of things to come?

Milo appeared in the doorway. "Dillon, I'm glad you're here." He turned to Grace and pulled a chair from the old table in the corner. "Sit down, honey."

Something in her husband's tone sounded ominous. "What's wrong?" She searched his face with growing alarm.

"The county sheriff was just here. It seems Reuben has disappeared." Milo massaged his temples.

Dillon stepped closer to his father. "What do you mean?"

"Your brother rode up to the mountain yesterday and hasn't been heard from since."

Grace slid into the nearest chair and stared at the steam rising from the coffeepot on the stove. She looked again at her husband, hoping he would tell her it was just a bad joke. His face was pale.

"Reuben and Duke weren't going to put in fishing camp until next week," Dillon protested.

"Must have changed their minds." Milo put an arm around his wife. "Duke was found at the bottom of a ravine. He was shot in the back."

Grace gasped.

"He's alive, but in a coma." Milo's words sounded tinny and hollow to Grace. "That's not all. The sheriff wants Reuben for questioning."

CHAPTER 4

I may stand alone,
But I would not change my free thoughts for a throne.
Lord Byron

Geneva, Switzerland
Friday, June 9

Anna O'Neil stepped from the stretch limo and ascended the restaurant's marble steps. At the top she was greeted by a maître d'. "Madame, it is an honor to serve you this evening—an extraordinary honor indeed."

Anna felt her face redden, and her fingers rose to her cheek as if she could brush away the embarrassment. Last night's speech at the Earth Summit had made her an instant celebrity—not what Anna had in mind when she chose her career. "Thank you." She smiled graciously, feeling a bit like a fraud. The highbrow social life was not for her. Bare feet in a cool stream, tattered blue jeans, and the latest copy of *The Wildlife Journal*—that was more Anna's speed.

"Your party is waiting, Ms. O'Neil." The maître d' serpentined past burgundy chairs and walnut tables that glistened with silver and crystal settings. Heads turned. The opulent room came alive with conversation as Anna strolled past, wearing a simple mid-length black dress and a single strand of pearls.

From the head of a long table near the window, media mogul Randolph Harrington rose slightly as his guest of honor approached. "Anna O'Neil!" He enunciated her name for emphasis. "I am so pleased that you could join us."

Anna took her seat beside a tall, thin girl barely in her twenties. She recognized the flawless face from the grocery store tabloids. This fashion model was the new Mrs. Harrington. "Lily, isn't it?"

The young bride nodded politely, then shyly looked away.

Randolph presented Anna to his other guests, making introductions down the long table. His distinguished friends included a French diplomat, a movie star and her male-model companion, an explorer, and an international banker. The names became a blur to Anna, except one: Gabor Gagne, founder of the Endangered Earth Alliance.

"I can't believe I finally get to meet you, Mr. Gagne." Anna fought a sudden rush of insecurity. "I've been an admirer for years. Your work in the field of ecology has been an inspiration to me."

"That's kind of you to say," he said with a toss of his salt-and-pepper hair. "A high compliment coming from you."

Laugh lines framed Gabor's brown eyes—an image captured on the cover of last month's *Time* magazine. Anna felt like a star-struck school girl. "Congratulations on being named Man of the Year," she said, wiping sticky palms discreetly on her napkin.

Gabor smiled. "The article was flattering," he said, his words soft. "But really—I'm only one small gear in the machinery of change."

Anna recognized the quote from the magazine article. "I know what you mean, Mr. Gagne."

"Please, call me Gabor." He studied Anna. "I was moved by your speech last night. You're articulate and knowledgeable. My organization needs gifted people like you. There is a top-level position available on my team."

Anna could not believe her ears. The founder of the Endangered Earth Alliance was offering her a job. "I don't know what to say."

Gabor handed her a business card. "Think about it and get back to me next week."

Aware that the other dinner guests were staring, Anna offered an impish smile. "It seems Mr. Gagne and I are members of the same mutual admiration society." Laughter trickled down the long table.

"Whatever you call it," Randolph Harrington interjected, "it is well deserved." With a crisp snap of his fingers, the media mogul summoned their waiter and instructed him to pour the chilled champagne.

Anna held up her hand when he got to her. "No, thanks. I don't drink."

"I insist, if only for the sake of a toast." Randolph nodded to the waiter, who complied.

Across the table, Lily Harrington turned her head, staring out the window at the twinkling lights of Geneva.

Anna noted the sadness on the young woman's face and wondered what a supermodel, married to one of the wealthiest men in the world, could be unhappy about. Ashamed of her thoughts, Anna reminded herself that the true treasures of life are not for sale.

Lily Harrington swept her gaze toward Anna, almost as though she had sensed her musings. The model brushed a strand of silky sable-colored hair from her face and smiled. Against a backdrop of perfect porcelain skin, her green eyes were deep and probing.

Ting, ting, ting. The sound of silver tapping crystal resonated from Randolph's direction, summoning the table's attention. After a few moments, with all eyes fixed on him, he lifted his champagne glass. "Join me in a toast to the extraordinary Anna O'Neil." He looked at his guest of honor. "To our paragon of green virtue, our new diva of environmental ethics!"

Crystal goblets kissed over linen. Anna cringed at the attention and pretended to take a sip.

Soon the other guests returned to their respective

conversations and Randolph leaned close to Anna. "I'm sure you are aware of my efforts in the media."

"Yes, of course," she replied, doing a mental inventory. Three blockbuster movies with a decidedly green message, a series of eco documentaries, and last but not least, the Green Ranger cartoon and its spawn of best-selling action heroes. "You have been a champion for the cause."

Randolph puffed up like a sage grouse in full strut. "In this elite ministry of enlightenment, we are fellow soldiers. It is a difficult battle, but if we're going to change the culture of ignorance, we must keep our eyes on the prize: a glorious, thriving ecosystem free from the ravages of mankind." He raised his glass again and the table followed his lead. "We are making progress, but there is much to be done."

Anna opened her mouth to respond but decided against it. She had heard such high-concept eco speak before—it made her uncomfortable.

The waiter returned and placed a chilled bowl of vichyssoise before each guest.

"I have taken the liberty of ordering for everyone," Randolph announced. He paused as the waiter unfolded his napkin and placed it on his lap. "I'm sure my dinner selection will be more than satisfactory." He looked around. "Now, shall we get down to business?" Without waiting for a response, Randolph pressed on. "Anna, I am intrigued by the possibility of making a movie about your life. The young people of our great planet must have their heroes and role models, don't you agree?"

Surprised by the abrupt announcement, Anna felt mildly annoyed. It seemed like manipulation wrapped in flatteries.

As though the matter was settled, Randolph lifted a spoonful of soup to his thin lips. "Oh, yes . . ." he paused, holding the spoon level. "Did I mention that Lily and I have just become the proud owners of a twenty-thousand-acre tract in the beautiful Pristine Valley where you live?"

"Oh?" Anna took a sip of water.

"It's located near the head of Fischer Creek, bordering the wilderness."

Prime elk migration territory, Anna thought disapprovingly. "I know the spot. But isn't it owned by the Wildlife Conservatory?"

Randolph laughed. "Let's just say I had a rather large tract of land in the Sierra Nevadas and the conservatory was interested in a trade. Anyway, for a few weeks each summer, we shall be neighbors. In fact, construction of our little cabin has already begun."

Lily looked at her husband and wrinkled her brow. "You told the contractor you wanted at least ten thousand square feet of space, but I never heard you say anything about a cabin."

"It was just a figure of speech," he snapped.

Lily grew quiet and stared at the napkin in her lap.

Anna leaned toward the young model. "I look forward to getting to know you."

Lily's face brightened. "Will you be returning to Wyoming right away?"

"No. I've made plans to spend time with my father off the coast of Maine first." In her mind, Anna visualized the rugged shore and could almost smell the brisk salt air of the Atlantic.

"Off the coast?" Lily asked.

"A place called Canaan Island," Anna said. "It's been in our family for generations. We keep a summer home there." Her thoughts turned to her father. For days, she had tried to reach him, to no avail. It was not like Malcolm to go away without letting her know. Anna pushed her bowl of soup aside. Anxiety had overshadowed her appetite. Maybe the island's phone was down again. In a few days, she would probably see Malcolm face to face and laugh about her worries.

"Randolph!" Lily cried. "What's wrong?"

Anna's eyes shot across the table to the host, who was slouched forward, head in hands.

"Randolph?" his young wife repeated, clutching his shoulder.

The billionaire lifted his ashen face. Small beads of sweat appeared on Randolph's forehead. "I'm fine. Just tired." He pushed himself up from the table and mustered an unconvincing smile. "If you will excuse us, it's been a long day. Please enjoy your meal."

Anna joined the other guests as they echoed their respects.

Gabor stood and offered to help, but Randolph brushed aside the gesture. The invincible Randolph Harrington looked fragile as he shuffled away, leaning on his young bride for support. An awkward silence settled across the table.

"I'm sure he'll be okay," Gabor Gagne said. He raised his glass in a toast. "To Randolph Harrington and his legacy."

"Green revolution!" someone at the far end of the table called out.

"Revolution!" everyone replied. Everyone except Anna.

CHAPTER 6

Life treads on life, and heart on heart,
We press too close, in church and mart,
To keep a dream or grave apart.
Elizabeth Barrett Browning

Wyoming
Friday, June 9

Grace stepped through the doors of the Cedar Ridge hospital, still trying to process the events that had brought her there. Duke Bassett had been shot in the back. Her oldest son, Reuben, was missing in the mountains, possibly hurt, maybe worse. Grace shuddered as she pushed the elevator button and tried to calm herself. She couldn't think of this now. Cassandra and Cordell needed her.

Grace emerged from the elevator and found Cassandra and her grandson in the waiting room. "Oh, honey," she said and wrapped her ample arms around her daughter-in-law. Cassandra stiffened.

"I'm glad you came, Grandma," Cordell said, volunteering a hug.

"You've grown two inches since the last time I saw you!" Grace tried to recall when that was. She turned to Cassandra. "How is Duke?"

"Dad's in a coma," her daughter-in-law said flatly. "The doctors don't know if he'll recover."

"What happened?"

Cassandra's lips shrank into a pout. "I suppose we'll find out soon. A special investigative team from Cheyenne arrived a few hours ago. They're at the ranch now, going through Reuben's things, especially the guns and rifle shells."

"This doesn't make any sense," Grace said. Tears filled her eyes. "They should be out looking for Reuben. He could be injured too."

"Oh, they want to find him all right." Cassandra showed no emotion. "There's something you need to know about your son. Reuben has been . . . Well, let's just say he's changed."

"What are you talking about?" Grace felt her blood pressure rise as she watched her daughter-in-law pace the room.

"Frankly," Cassandra said tersely, "I don't know what my husband is capable of!"

"Oh, honey, you can't mean that. You don't think that Reuben . . . He loves your father."

"Dad wouldn't hurt anyone," Cordell protested.

Cassandra flashed a smug smile. "Love can be blind, can't it, Grace? But someone had to be straight with the investigators when they asked if Reuben has ever been . . . unstable."

"That's a lie!" Cordell shouted. His young face twisted with anger and he glared at his mother. "I can't believe you said that!"

Grace took a step and reached for her grandson, but he bolted from the waiting room and disappeared down the hallway.

"It was nice of you to come," Cassandra said in a strained voice. "But I think we can manage without you." She selected a magazine, snapped it open, and plopped into a chair.

Grace stood in stunned silence, clutching her purse so hard her knuckles felt numb. "I'll be praying for your father."

Cassandra offered her mother-in-law a feeble good-bye.

In the hallway, Grace looked in vain for her grandson, longing to comfort him. She left, feeling sad and helpless. The mood stayed with her as she drove back home to Fischer Creek.

In her cabin, Grace made a cup of tea to calm her nerves. Her hands shook when she poured the steaming water from the kettle. She should have braced herself for such a confrontation, but given the circumstances, she had hoped Cassandra would at least be civil.

She took a sip, wondering why things had grown so complicated with her daughter-in-law. Reuben married late in life and Grace was delighted when he settled down with the rancher's daughter. The Fischers welcomed Cassandra into the family. But after the marriage, things began to change. Grace recalled how her daughter-in-law grew moody and possessive. When Cordell was born, Cassandra cast aside all pretense and seemed determined to drive a wedge between her husband and his family.

Grace rarely saw her oldest son, except on the few occasions when he stopped by the Fischer Creek Café. During those precious visits, Grace would pour Reuben a steaming mug of coffee and banter cheerfully about old times while pretending not to notice the sadness in his eyes.

Grace had never understood her daughter-in-law's jealous tantrums, yet she had always assumed that Cassandra loved her son—that is, until tonight.

In her tiny kitchen, amid the clutter of mementos, Grace lifted a pair of white china ducks and held them in her hand. Reuben had given them to her for Christmas when he was eight years old. He had saved his allowance for weeks to buy them.

The weight of the years fell heavily upon her. Grace felt old. She rested her weary head on her arms and closed her eyes.

From the other end of the cabin, she heard Milo's rhythmic snoring.

"Lord, please help Reuben. Bring him back home to those who care for him." She lifted her eyes to the blackness of the window. Somewhere out there, her firstborn was in trouble. The moon, barely a sliver of white, could not light an owl's way, but Grace grasped hope with a maternal fist. *If anyone could survive in the wilderness,* she told herself, *Reuben would find a way.*

CHAPTER 6

Oh why should the spirit of mortal be proud?
Like a fast-flitting meteor, a fast-flying cloud,
A flash of the lightning, a break of the wave,
He passes from life to his rest in the grave.
    William Knox

Maine
Monday, June 12

Sleep eluded Anna on the flight from Geneva to New York. She felt claustrophobic and restless. Sandwiched between slumbering strangers, the long, dark hours passed slowly with a serenade of tinny music issuing through the cheap headsets. Anna blamed the unyielding airline seats for her insomnia, yet it was her own turbulent thoughts that kept her tossing and turning in discontent.

By the time the 777 touched down in New York, Anna was beyond tired. Floating on adrenaline and a double shot of Starbucks espresso purchased in the airport, she boarded the short commuter flight to Bangor, Maine.

When Anna finally merged onto the toll road in her rental car, it was almost 10:30 AM. She fell in line with the rush-hour crawl and punched her father's number on her cell phone. It rang and rang. In a burst of frustration, Anna tossed the phone on the seat beside her and zipped through openings in the traffic, finally turning south toward Camden. The road was relatively clear. Anna pushed the throttle, accelerating past familiar childhood landmarks of white-steepled churches, immaculate brick row houses, and sunny roadside antique markets. These images, normally taken in slow and easy like a savored scent, were lost on her now.

Anna stopped only once along the way, at Jeanie's Road House Café, a quaint greasy spoon that had become a traditional halfway point to Canaan Island. The young waitress, clad in mismatched T-shirt, flowered skirt and striped tights, popped her chewing gum and scribbled Anna's order on a notepad. She returned shortly with a cup of apple cider and a blueberry scone.

Anna stared at the food with a dwindling appetite. Her mind was on Malcolm, lying ill or injured for all she knew. Anna pushed the plate aside and summoned the waitress, who was slapping crumbs from the counter with a dirty rag. "I'm going to take this order to go."

The girl scowled, working her gum over. "You want the cider in a paper cup?"

Anna nodded, wrapped the scone in a napkin, and

stood. She placed a generous tip on the table and settled the bill.

One hour and twelve minutes later, Anna's car was bouncing down a fir-lined access road. Rounding the last rutted curve, the scenery blossomed with a breathtaking view of the Atlantic's gray-blue waters. A half mile from shore, the long arm of Canaan Island reached out as if to welcome Anna home.

She found Malcolm's BMW parked in its usual spot on the far side of the boathouse and pulled in next to it. With as much speed as she could muster, Anna removed her luggage and tossed it into one of the extra aluminum boats.

She fired up the outboard with three pulls of the cord. Anna cut through the swift channel currents that ran between the island and the shore. Maneuvering the craft around Canaan's point, she followed the shoreline east, past granite cliffs, small sandy beaches, and hilly stands of pines. Each place nurtured a memory. "My backyard," Anna said aloud, recalling cool summer days filled with nature's wonder.

By the time the dock came into view, Anna had convinced herself that her fretting had been nothing more than a delayed response to the recent excitement. She cut the outboard motor and drifted to the short, weathered dock. There she tossed a rope over the mooring, secured the boat, and with her bags in hand, jumped from the dock to the shore. She stepped gingerly on the barnacle-covered boulders and drew in a deep breath of salt air. Anna bolted up the hillside like an eager child.

The O'Neil family's two-story summer home rose into view like a towering Gothic monument. The sight of its pink granite walls and steep gabled roof revived years of memories and a strong sense of place. Anna scanned the arched windows for a glimpse of Malcolm's face. Her gaze settled on the tarnished copper door. She expected him to fly across the threshold with arms open, as he had done so many times before. But that didn't happen.

Finding the front door unlocked, Anna pushed it open and called Malcolm's name. Silence. She lifted the phone's receiver. Her spirits sank at the sound of the dial tone. Beside the phone, the answering machine blinked with messages—most of them hers, no doubt. She would get to them later.

After a quick sweep of the big empty house, Anna was more worried than ever. Malcolm's things were in his room and signs of his presence were everywhere, including a half-read book lying open beside his favorite leather chair and a clutter of correspondence strewn upon the kitchen table. Most disturbing of all was the void Anna felt. The house seemed empty and hollow.

With her heart pounding, she ran outside and hurried along a well-trodden path, calling her father's name. Panic turned to desperation as she combed Malcolm's favorite spots. She fought hard to dam her tears. He could be anywhere on the forty-nine-acre island.

Frustration turned to stubborn determination. Anna pressed on, watching for movement and searching the thickets. She startled a raccoon, but there was no sign of Malcolm.

Anna headed back to the house, scanning the rugged coastline as she went. A cluster of seals basked in the sun on a rock just off the point. *Think,* she told herself, trying to pinpoint places where Malcolm would go. It would be dark in a few hours.

Near the shore, a noisy flock of black-backed gulls fluttered and screeched greedily over a mound of seaweed that had washed up beside a boulder. Anna wanted to scream in frustration at the ill-mannered scavenger birds.

A faint, sickening odor rose to her nostrils, growing stronger with each step. It was the smell of fish and seaweed . . . and death. Fear crept up Anna's spine. Forgetting to breathe, she turned back to the beach.

Twenty yards away, Anna saw the body of a man lying in a tangle of green seaweed, half buried in the sand. The dimming light mercifully hid most of the swollen corpse from view.

Anna dropped to her knees. "Oh, God, no!" she cried. In an act of violent protest, she scooped up fists of gravel and sand and hurled it at the sea birds. Anna's stomach turned sour. She scrambled to her feet and stumbled blindly to the house on rubbery legs.

With trembling hands, she punched three numbers on the kitchen wall phone. "Help me!" A deep, guttural cry escaped from her lips. "I've just found a body." The words caught in Anna's throat. "I think it's my father."

—⁓—

Tuesday, June 13

Anna's eyes were swollen and bone dry from all the crying. She still could not believe her father was gone. She sat in an overstuffed chair and watched with surreal detachment as Port Williwaught's investigative team poked about the house, dusting for prints, taking photos, and opening drawers. Light filtered through the tall windows, illuminating dust motes that had remained undisturbed through the long winter months. Reminders of Anna's loss were everywhere, real and fresh; the book that Malcolm had been reading, the slippers beside her father's bed, and on the kitchen table lay a newspaper with the missing piece torn from its page.

Unbidden, the memory of Malcolm, lying in a tangle of seaweed, floated back to her mind. Anna shuddered. Her stomach turned rancid.

"When was the last time you had contact with your father, Ms. O'Neil?" asked an older man dressed in plain street clothes. He stood beside her chair, ran his hand over a crop of course dark hair, and observed Anna with keen black eyes aimed down a hawkish nose.

"I spoke with Malcolm about three weeks ago," she said weakly.

The man rubbed the five o'clock shadow on his weathered face. "Did you always call your father Malcolm?"

"For as long as I can remember."

"Would you characterize your relationship as close?"

"Yes, very."

He nodded, and wrote something in a small spiral notebook.

"I'm afraid I've already forgotten your name," Anna said.

"That's not unusual in these circumstances." His voice carried faint cords of compassion. "Investigator Jay Corpizio, with the Maine State Police."

Anna gazed out the window at the Atlantic. The constant rhythms of nature brought a measure of comfort, or was it escape? *I am an orphan,* she realized. Anna's mother had died when she was a toddler. Malcolm was all she had.

"How did my father die?" Her eyes brimmed with tears.

Investigator Corpizio looked at Anna as if trying to decide how much she was capable of hearing. "It looks like he was shot."

Anna felt as if she had been punched.

A man with a camera burst through the front door. "Sir, the crew's ready for pictures."

Corpizio nodded. He turned his attention back to

Anna. "Did your father own a gun?"

"No." She thrust herself from the chair and stood face to face with Corpizio. "Did you see the note in the kitchen?"

He flipped the pages of his notebook. "Yes. We've taken it as evidence."

"I don't understand why Malcolm wrote it." A wave of emotion swamped Anna as she recalled the words Malcolm had scribbled on the border of the morning paper. *Happy birthday, little Anna.* In the wake of recent events, it seemed like a cruel joke. "It makes no sense," she said. "My birthday was six months ago."

The investigator cocked his head with interest. "That is curious." Corpizio scribbled something and looked back at Anna. "The bottom half of the note was torn away. Do you have any idea where it is?"

Anna blinked. "No."

Investigator Corpizio cleared his throat. "It wasn't found on the body."

A shudder snaked down her spine. Anna rubbed her arms and sat down again.

"You arrived well after your father's death; is that correct?"

"I just flew in from Switzerland a few hours ago."

"I know. We checked with the airlines and car rental in Bangor."

The idea that she could be considered a suspect both surprised and offended Anna. She crossed her arms defensively.

"We will need a list of his associates, friends, and enemies."

"Enemies?" Anna's throat constricted. "My father was well liked. I don't know of anyone who would want to hurt him." Nevertheless, someone did hurt him.

"Was your father in the habit of going for a walk in his pajamas?"

Anna's head started swimming. "I don't feel very well."

"I understand." The investigator reached out to offer a steady hand, but she refused the gesture. "Is there anyone you would like me to call?"

"No." She moved toward the hallway. "I'd like to rest now."

In her room, Anna moved to the inglenook and lit a fire, then collapsed upon her antique sleigh bed. For what seemed like an eternity, she lay staring up at the ceiling, willing sleep to take her to a better place. But sleep refused to come.

The dam broke and tears rolled down her cheeks. "I can't believe this has happened."

The investigator's words had unsettled Anna. Malcolm would never go out into the cold Atlantic air without at least throwing on a pair of jeans. Anna pulled an afghan around her chilled body. Obviously, he had fled the house in a hurry. Thoughts of her father's last moments tormented Anna. Where did he go in the moments before he died? Had he suffered? Sadness crept beneath the covers and settled about her like a lead weight as one question in particular taunted her. *Why?*

CHAPTER 7

Our hearts, our hopes, are all with thee,
Our hearts, our hopes, our prayers, our tears,
Our faith, triumphant o'er our fears,
Are all with thee!
Henry Wadsworth Longfellow

Wyoming
Sunday, June 18

"You'll be fine," Grace Fischer said to her husband. "The gravy's on the stove, next to a pitcher of pancake batter. Biscuits are warming in the oven, along with a pan of ham and bacon. All you have to do is fry the eggs."

"I always break the yolks," Milo said with a pout. He retrieved a mug from a cupboard and slammed the door. "I don't know how you expect me to tend to the customers and do the cooking, too," he squawked.

Grace chewed on her lip. The dreaded moment had finally arrived. She had to tell Milo that Dillon's wife would be stopping by to lend a hand. "I know it can be difficult to juggle things alone, especially if it gets busy. So as soon as Jody drops Christy at summer school . . ."

"Jody?" Milo exploded. "Don't tell me she's coming to help. That girl is as nervous as a drop of water in a hot skillet. Makes me tired just being in the same room with her."

"I know," Grace placated. "But for heavens sake, you need the help. And let's face it, Jody's got the energy of three waitresses."

"We wouldn't be havin' this discussion if you didn't have your head set on going to church," Milo said.

Before Grace could respond, the back door sprang open and Dillon's wife blew in like a zephyr. "Sorry I'm late. The alarm didn't go off this morning. Christy threw a fit 'cause I was out of Fruit Loops and only had Cheerios. She loves Fruit Loops. Can't keep 'em around. Dillon forgot to put gas in the car and I wasn't sure I'd make it. But here I am!" Jody pealed a light jacket from her skinny frame and tossed it on a hook near the door. "I'm ready to start."

Grace cautioned Milo with a look, grabbed her things, and kissed her daughter-in-law's warm cheek. "Thanks for coming."

"Oh, I'm glad to help," Jody said. "I had a lot to do at home, of course—laundry, vacuuming, and I was thinking of baking some bread. But this is more fun." Jody turned to Milo. "We can catch up on things; I have so much to talk about."

Ignoring Milo's imploring eyes, Grace slipped through the door. It had been years since she'd attended church. Something, it seemed, always came up and "next Sunday" turned to next month, and then next spring. Before Grace realized it, a year had passed, and another.

She stepped boldly out the door, determined that nothing was going to keep her away this Sunday morning.

Fifteen minutes later, Grace steered their Subaru wagon down a little dirt road to the Church of the Rock. She parked beside the old converted barn, the first to arrive.

She found the door unlocked. Inside, the cavernous room encased the morning chill. Grace pulled her sweater around her neck. She selected a seat in the back row among the mismatched chairs and glanced around. Despite a few colorful Scripture banners and a makeshift kitchenette, the building still looked like an old barn. Little birds chattered in the rafters and flitted about the old wooden cross, which hung above the pulpit. Grace noticed a bird nest in the crook of the crossbar.

"Did you know none of those little guys can fall to the ground without God knowing about it?"

Grace turned to see Pastor Charlie Waits standing behind her.

"It's in the book of Matthew. Jesus said, 'Don't be afraid. You are worth more than many sparrows.'" The pastor laid his hand on Grace's shoulder and gave it a reassuring squeeze. "I've been praying for Duke, Reuben, and the rest of your family."

Grace found comfort in her old friend's words. "Thanks, Charlie."

He looked serene and full of faith. His brown Native American eyes reflected gentleness and light. Charlie Waits was a changed man, as close to a miracle as Grace had ever come. If God could turn Charlie's life around, surely he could bring Reuben home again. Grace needed to believe that.

A small crowd trickled into the building and church was soon under way. Pastor Charlie began the service with prayer in his native Crow tongue and followed with a translation: "Lord, teach our feet to walk in Your ways, teach our hands to reach for You in the night, teach our hearts to know, love, and trust You in all circumstances. Amen."

In the front row, someone strummed a guitar and the congregation slid into a folksy rendition of "A Mighty Fortress Is Our God," followed by a few other old hymns.

Near the end of worship, the door opened and a latecomer slipped into the sanctuary. He moved to the back row, leaving a half dozen empty seats between himself and Grace. The stranger slouched low in a seat and folded his arms across his chest. Grace recognized him as the young man she had seen outside the café a few days earlier. Native American—maybe Crow nation, Grace figured, noting his long braids and patterned shirt.

His dark, narrowed eyes stared straight ahead.

When the last song faded, the pastor lowered his head in prayer. He opened a tattered Bible and placed it on the makeshift podium.

The pastor instructed the congregation to open their Bibles to the book of Romans. "It says here that from the beginning of the world, God's invisible qualities have been seen. How? This beautiful earth reflects His beauty. What's more—He lets us enjoy it!" Charlie paused and silence settled over the room. "But here's the sad thing. Most people can't bring themselves to thank God for His thoughtful gifts." The pastor folded his brown hands on the makeshift podium and looked earnestly at the congregation. He stepped down from the platform and moved to the barn doors.

All eyes followed Charlie as he lifted a board from the latch and pushed on the aging wood. Rusty hinges groaned as the double doors parted. Fresh air spilled into the barn, along with the rich aroma of sweet grass and crisp blue spruce.

A beautiful view opened before the congregation: sun-drenched meadows where new blades of timothy hay peeked through last year's refuse. In the distance, a tangle of orange willows lined a river that meandered near the base of a steep cliff.

"Some people think this mountain can help them find the answers they seek. I was once one of them." Charlie sighed. "I thought I'd figured out the meaning of life without God's help—just me and nature."

The pastor turned back to face the congregation. "If you built a beautiful house, you would expect your family to appreciate the work you did. But, what if you overheard your family talking to the house, saying, 'House, you are so beautiful. How did you build yourself? You are so mysterious; I am in total awe of you. You give me shelter. You give me warmth. You give me joy. Because of all this, you are worthy of my worship and praise. In fact, beautiful and mysterious house, since I live here, I must be a part of you. I will call you Mother.'"

Someone in the congregation yelled, "I'd have 'em all committed." Laughter shot through the room.

"I wonder if God has ever felt that way about us," Charlie said as he returned to the podium.

The people considered the question in silence.

"Let's pray." He bowed his head. "Lord, You formed the heavens and the earth. You spoke, and they were created. You loved us enough to show us the way back to You. Help us to see the truth, to love the truth, and to honor You. Amen."

The young Native American in the back row muttered something. Grace couldn't make out the words, but the tone was caustic. The stranger stood abruptly, knocking over his chair in the process. Heads turned.

"What are you freaks lookin' at?" he snarled. Like a cornered animal, he scurried out the door, leaving Grace to wonder what had caused this burst of anger.

—ᴍ—

Sunday, June 18

Peter fled from the church and didn't stop until he reached Cedar Ridge's main street. There, he lingered in front of a storefront, staring at a display of Indian artifacts and handcrafted items—pieces of his heritage. In the glass, the ghost of his reflection stared back. His expression darkened. "I don't belong here," he mumbled. No one in this one-stoplight town would even give him a job application. *"Not hiring right now"* was the mantra. Peter knew better. He saw the way they all looked at him.

A steady flow of cars caravanned down the main street, making it impossible to cross the road. Most of the license plates were out of state, Peter noted.

"Look, Mommy, a real Indian!" A little boy pointed his rubber tomahawk in Peter's direction. The child's mother offered an apologetic grimace and tugged the toddler down the sidewalk.

"Tourist town," Peter said under his breath and flicked a bitter look in the direction from which he had come. "A tourist town with a joke for a pastor."

Peter's stomach growled and he remembered a coffee shop on one of the side streets. He sank his hand into the pocket of his jeans and pulled out the contents: a few bills, some coins, a book of matches, and an old, tattered photograph. Peter stared at the image on the snapshot for a moment. Anger percolated deep inside his soul. Peter shoved the items back into his pocket, shifted the weight of his backpack, and trudged on.

CHAPTER 8

Have mercy on me, O LORD, for I am in trouble;
My eye wastes away with grief,
Yes; my soul and my body!
Psalm 31:9

Maine
Monday, June 19

For the first time in a week, Anna emerged from her grief long enough to take in her surroundings. The rooms at the Lobster Inn hadn't seen a new coat of paint in years and the walls were covered with cheap ocean prints, but it was the best lodging Port Williwaught had to offer. She sat on the corner of her mattress and ran her hand over the faded bedding. It would have to do, at least until the forensic team had left the island. Investigator Corpizio said it would be a couple of days at the most before Anna could return to Canaan Island without fear of contaminating the evidence.

She picked up a magazine and thumbed through its

pages. One headline caught her interest. "Fight to Preserve Alaska's Wilderness from Drilling." The first line of the article mentioned the Endangered Earth Alliance. Anna sat up. Gabor Gagne! The job offer! She launched to her feet, retrieved her backpack from the closet, and dumped its contents on the bed. "That business card has to be in here somewhere." Anna checked every pocket, but the only card she found was from Randolph Harrington Enterprises. She worked up her courage and dialed. To her surprise, the receptionist immediately transferred the call to the mogul's office.

"Anna, how are you? Lily and I feel simply horrible about the news—such an atrocious loss."

"You heard about my father's death?"

"I read all about it in the *New York Times*. Your father was an outstanding columnist. I admired his strong environmental convictions."

"Thanks," Anna said softly.

"If there's anything Lily and I can do, anything at all . . ."

"Actually, I was wondering if you have the contact information for Gabor Gagne."

"Ah, yes. The job offer."

"I've decided to turn it down, under the circumstances." Anna hesitated. "I just . . ."

"No need to offer an explanation," Randolph said. "I'm sure Gabor will understand. I shall be speaking with him in the next day or so. If you'd like, I could pass on your regrets."

Anna sighed with relief. "That would be wonderful."

"There must be a million family details shouting for your attention." He paused, "Will you be keeping the island? I mean, in light of your father's murder."

Anna squeezed her eyes shut and fought a wave of grief. "It's been in our family for generations. I haven't decided."

Suddenly, she felt tethered to the telephone cord. "It was nice talking to you, Randolph. Please give Lily my regards." Anna hung up, feeling weak beneath the crushing weight of her emotions.

—ᘯᘯ—

Los Angeles
Monday, June 19

Lily walked two steps behind her husband as Randolph strutted down the corridor of his corporate headquarters.

"Did I mention that Anna O'Neil phoned?" he asked. "I'm sure she is devastated by her father's untimely demise. I've decided to make a generous donation to a charity in Malcolm O'Neil's name."

Lily nodded, but her thoughts were back at the doctor's office. Randolph's physician had seemed concerned. She reassured herself that it was nothing serious and tried to keep up with her husband's stride. He looked healthy enough, though maybe a little tired. "How do you feel?" she asked.

Randolph shot his wife an annoyed look. "Never better."

Heads turned in the media center as Randolph passed by.

"Good morning, Mr. Harrington," his underlings chanted, as though hungry for a scrap of recognition.

Lily empathized with the employees, those poor invisible people. There were times when she wondered if Randolph truly saw her.

Her husband turned down a short corridor lined with original Ansel Adams photographs. At the end, a handsome, solidly built woman nodded respectfully from behind a shiny black marble desk.

"Mrs. Harrington, how nice to see you." The secretary smiled like a Cheshire cat.

Before Lily could respond, Randolph snapped his fingers. "Come along, Wildflower." He opened a solid mahogany door and ushered her inside.

Randolph punched the intercom button and uttered one word: "Schedule."

"You have a full day, Mr. Harrington," the secretary announced. "There's a 9:00 AM meeting with Craig Jarvis."

"Who?"

"The new CEO of NBC. He wants to discuss a possible syndication agreement regarding the Green Ranger cartoon."

"Why isn't Ray working on this?" Randolph demanded.

"Mr. Jarvis insisted on meeting with you, sir. At 10, you have a board of directors meeting, followed by the World Foundation planning forum." She paused briefly to draw a breath. "The private screening of *The Whales of the Blue* is at 2:00 PM. The actors will be there. Each celebrity is expected to present the Endangered Earth Alliance with a check. The media will also be on site, of course. You're free at 4:30, but Dr. Reisen called and said he needs to see you. Would you like me to make an appointment with him, sir?"

Lily fought a growing sense of foreboding.

"No. Get Reisen on the phone."

"Would you like to hear the remainder of your schedule first?"

"That can wait." Randolph hung up and drummed his fingers on his desk. Lily followed his gaze to the full-length windows, which displayed a spectacular view of Los Angeles.

The intercom buzzed. Harrington lurched forward and pressed the button. "Your doctor is on the line, sir."

Randolph punched the flashing button on the speakerphone. "Yes?"

The physician cleared his throat. "The test results just came in. "I'd like go over them with you."

"I'm listening."

"I'd rather not talk about my findings over the

phone."

"I have neither the time nor the patience for this, Reisen. If you have something to discuss with me, just say it!"

The doctor hesitated. "Very well. Your granulocyte level is forty times the norm. As I explained to you when we drew the blood, granulocytes are a type of white blood cell."

"So I'm anemic?"

"Yes, but that's not all."

Randolph froze. "Go ahead."

"You have leukemia. I would like to admit you to the hospital as soon as possible. After further testing, I'll be able to tell you more."

Lily watched the color fade from her husband's face and she moved to his side to offer comfort.

Randolph's face remained rigid and his voice controlled. "I'll get back to you on this," he said and ended the call.

The intercom buzzed again. "Mr. Harrington, Craig Jarvis with NBC is here. Should I send him in?"

"No. Cancel all my appointments for today."

"But, sir, Mr. Jarvis . . ."

With a swift, angry movement, Randolph switched off the intercom. He paced to the wet bar, poured a brandy and moved to the window.

Lily followed her husband there. She reached for his trembling hand, but he pulled away from her touch.

Randolph stood as if he were alone—brooding, swirling his brandy, and gazing at the busy avenue below.

Down there, Lily thought with a hint of irony, life ebbed and flowed coldly, as though nothing had gone wrong—just like it had when she was a little girl and shuffled from one foster home to another.

"I'm scared." Randolph said. This time, his hand met Lily's. He squeezed so hard it hurt. "Wildflower, what am I going to do?"

Lily was stunned. It was almost inconceivable that anyone's opinion mattered to the great Randolph Harrington—least of all hers. Lily's heart surged with compassion. "We'll face this together," she said as her green eyes filled with tears.

CHAPTER 9

Though rashness can hope for but one result,
We are heedless, when fate draws nigh to us;
Adam Lindsay Gordon

Wyoming
Tuesday, June 20

Beneath a brilliant canopy of blue sky, Dillon drove through the town of Cedar Ridge in his old Chevy truck. The beautiful summer morning was lost on him. There was only one thing on his mind. Eleven days had passed since his brother, Reuben, had disappeared and Dillon wanted answers.

He pulled into the forest service parking lot and hopped out. The air was already hot for this time of day, and the new black asphalt felt soft beneath his boots. Dillon wiped a track of sweat from his neck, squared his shoulders, and marched inside.

The office clerk looked up from her work and rolled her eyes. "I'm sorry, Mr. Fischer," she droned, "but the Environmental Impact Statement on the logging hasn't come back and there have been no new developments regarding your brother since the last time you were here." The woman pulled a stack of forest service maps from the counter and straightened them.

Dillon gripped the counter and leaned forward. He felt the blood throbbing in his temples. "What do you mean, 'nothing new'? You haven't told me anything to begin with!"

"Is there a problem here?" The district ranger poked his head out his office door. His expression fell flat. "Oh, hello, Dillon." He stepped into the reception area. "We're doing everything we can to find Reuben."

"Yeah? Like what?"

"These things take time," the ranger said, rubbing a scraggly mustache. "We're a bit short staffed."

"Save it. I already know a special team of government trackers has come up from Cheyenne. Everybody in town is talking about it."

The ranger seemed both surprised and flustered by the disclosure. "The shooting of Duke Bassett is a criminal investigation. Of course we are very interested in talking to Reuben." He gave Dillon a long, sober look. "Anyone who attempts to aid or abet a suspect will be charged with obstructing justice."

"Is that a threat or a warning?" Dillon felt his face get hot and his fist curled.

The ranger's posture softened, but his words

remained firm. "Let us sort it out. That's my advice to you."

Dillon eyed the ranger with suspicion, not for what the man said, but what he had left out. Years of living in the shadow of federal land management policies had primed the pump of deep mistrust. *It's useless to press the issue,* Dillon thought as he slammed out the door. He would have to find the answers for himself.

—◊◊◊—

Tuesday, June 20

Dillon pulled into the Broken Arrow Ranch just before 2:00 PM. He drove past the lodge and backed the horse trailer into a parking space near the tack shed. He kicked up dust on the hard-trodden ground as he walked across the corral toward the cowhand. "Hey, Kip."

"I've been expecting you." The wrangler fired a string of tobacco through the slit in his front teeth, slipped on a pair of stained leather gloves, and ambled over to help unload the horses from Dillon's trailer.

After Dillon had tied the last horse to a fence post, he retrieved the tack and supplies from the back of his pickup and separated them into piles.

Kip drawled over small talk while they threw the packsaddles on the horses and loaded the panniers with supplies. Dillon wasn't listening. His thoughts were on the rugged terrain where his brother had vanished.

"Uncle Dillon!" Cordell appeared in the corral, breathing hard as if he'd been doing a fifty-yard sprint. "I'm going with you."

Dillon raised an eyebrow, then turned back to his task of straightening a halter. "Does your mom know about this?"

"Doesn't matter," the boy said. "If you're goin' up on the mountain to look for Dad, I'm coming too."

Dillon threw a blanket and saddle on his mare and tightened the cinch. He tied his long duster jacket on the back of the saddle and patted his shirt pocket to make sure he had matches.

The boy turned to Kip. "Would you wrangle up a fresh horse and help me get it saddled?"

The old man's leathery lips parted to expose a gaping tobacco-stained grin. He pulled a halter from a peg and disappeared.

"I'm going with you, Uncle Dillon." Cordell stood defiantly in front of him.

"I don't think that's such a good idea." Dillon threw the panniers across the mule's packsaddle.

"He's my dad." Cordell's young face flashed with emotion.

The wrangler returned with a gelding. Before he could tie the animal to a hitch, Cordell threw a blanket across its back and retrieved a saddle from the tack shed.

Cassandra thrust open the corral gate. Her eyes narrowed and popped with rage. "What is going on here?"

Dillon did his best to ignore his sister-in-law. He busied himself by shortening a stirrup.

"Who gave you permission to park your trailer here? This is private property!"

"For cryin' out loud, Cassandra, your husband is missing," Dillon said. "Can't you give it a rest?"

She stomped over to her brother-in-law and leaned uncomfortably close. Dillon felt her hot breath on his face, but he stood his ground.

"You're trespassing. If you don't leave, I'll have you arrested." A smile spasmed at the corners of Cassandra's mouth, but her eyes held no humor.

"No, you won't, Mom," Cordell interjected. "I gave him permission to be here."

Cassandra whirled around to face her son. "What did you say?"

"I'm going with Uncle Dillon and you're not standing in my way." He looked taller somehow as he stood up to his mother.

Cassandra watched her son struggle to maneuver the bridle over the horse's nose. She let loose a burst of taunting laughter that stopped as abruptly as it had started. She took a brisk step forward and grabbed Cordell's arm. Her fingernails dug into his flesh. "You'll do what I tell you," she said with an eerie calm.

Cordell shook free from her grasp and turned back to the bridle. The horse finally accepted the bit, and Cordell fished the leather over the animal's ears.

Dillon watched quietly from under the brim of his baseball cap as he tied the last mule to the pack string.

Cassandra quivered. Her gaze slowly shifted in Dillon's direction and she pointed her finger at him like a rifle scope. "You take my son up on the mountain and I'll have charges brought against you."

"Yeah?" Cordell said as he mounted up. "You do that and you might just get a taste of your own medicine."

"What are you talking about?" Cassandra snapped.

He pulled up his sleeve to reveal deep gouge marks in his skin. "Don't they have child abuse laws in this state?"

A look of shock blazed across his mother's face. "You wouldn't dare."

"I've learned a lot from you."

Dillon untied his pack string, mounted, and gently kicked his horse into a trot. The sooner he got some distance from his sister-in-law, the better.

Behind him, he heard the sound of galloping hooves as Cordell closed the gap. His nephew, it seemed, had finally broken free.

From the crest of the mountain pass, Dillon searched the jagged terrain for a clue to his brother's disappearance. Far below, he spotted the ravine where Duke had been found. It was a wonder anyone could survive such a fall—especially with a bullet in the back.

"Does this trail get any worse?" Cordell asked, his voice tight with tension.

Dillon twisted in his saddle and looked back at his nephew. "This is the wide part." He grinned.

Cordell looked down. "There's hardly room enough for my horse's hooves." His gelding knocked a small boulder loose, sending a mini rockslide crackling down the steep slope. The boy paled.

"Guess that's why they call it "Say-Your-Prayers Pass," Dillon said. "Now, remember, if your horse loses his footing, you'll need to bail off. So I recommend you just dangle your feet out of your stirrups."

Cordell blinked nervously. "Do you think Dad and Grandpa came this way?"

"That's what we're here to find out." Dillon turned his attention back to what lay before him: miles and miles of wilderness. He fished a piece of butterscotch candy from his shirt pocket and popped it into his mouth. The afternoon was hotter than usual for this altitude and the dry, breezeless air was suffocating.

Dillon and Cordell followed the ridge, scanning the breaks for movement. They dropped over a knob and through a shaded umbrella of dense forest. After a short while, the trail widened between mountain currant bushes and tree moss that hung like tinsel from the pine trees. Sunlight trickled through blocks of shade and twinkled in the trail dust.

The shade felt good. Dillon removed his cap and ran a hand over a damp mop of hair.

A symphony of chatter rang out from the canopy.

"Hear that?" Dillon asked.

"Yeah. It sounds like Oz after Dorothy landed there."

Dillon raised his eyebrow.

"All the little creatures can see us, but we can't see them."

Before long, they came to a stream that meandered lazily along the edge of a small meadow. Dillon dismounted and tied his pack string to a lodge-pole pine. He was tired and thirsty, and his mouth felt caked with trail dust. "This looks like as good a place as any to stop for the night."

"I'm glad. My rear end feels like it's been pounded on the steel bed of a pickup truck."

"Sounds like you've been hanging around your grandpa too much."

"Not as much as I'd like," Cordell said bitterly.

"Did you bring a sleeping bag?

"Oh, man!" the teenager bellowed. "I'm so lame. What am I going to do?"

Dillon walked over to the packhorses. "Well, for starters, you can help me unpack. A good outfitter always takes care of the animals first."

They unfastened the ropes and rolled a tattered and stained piece of canvas off the back of the horse. Dillon went to work on the lash rope and threw a bedroll over the panniers. It hit Cordell on the head.

"When your old wrangler saw that you were bound

and determined to go, he threw an extra bedroll in for you."

"I could kiss good ol' Kip," Cordell exclaimed with the kind of exuberance only a fourteen-year-old boy can display.

Dillon shook his head. "You got a lot to learn, boy. Those are fightin' words to a wrangler."

"Well, he sure pulled my fat out of the fire," Cordell said over the top of the pack animal.

"Since you're feelin' your oats, you can lift that pannier and haul it over next to the other one. I'm gonna make a bear cache."

Cordell did as instructed while Dillon shimmied up a large pine and steadied himself at a wide fork in the tree. From there, he lowered the end of a rope and called for Cordell to tie it around a bundle of short lodge poles. Before long, a platform was firmly in place and the panniers of food securely out of reach of bears.

"You think caches really keep the bears away?" Cordell asked.

Dillon climbed down the tree and dropped to the ground. "Nope," he said. "Griz'll still be attracted to the smell, but they won't be able to get at it. It won't do much for sloppy campers who use their pants for napkins, though," he said with a wink.

"Forget about the food. Is there room up there for us?"

Dillon unrolled a canvas tent. "You don't need to

worry. See that mule?" He pointed to the animal grazing nearby. "Ol' Francis can sense a griz a mile away. If one gets close, she'll try to climb into our sleeping bags."

Before long, the tent was in place and the fire was crackling. First line of priority was a big pot of camp coffee before dinner. Jody had packed plenty of food, as usual. Dillon threw a slab of margarine into the crusty old frying pan, let it sizzle, and added a few thick pork chops. "Here," he said, handing Cordell a can of beans. "Open this."

The sun was fading fast over the horizon, but there was at least an hour of dusky light left.

Cordell struggled with the old-fashioned can opener. "Uncle Dillon," he asked, "what if Dad just had his fill of Mom? I mean . . .what if he just kinda cracked up?"

"You think that's what he did?" From under the bill of his cap, Dillon eyed his nephew.

The boy shook his head. "Sometimes I think Gramps and I were the only reasons he stuck around. Dad would never hurt Gramps and I'm pretty sure he wouldn't go off and leave me either." Cordell made the last turn of the can opener, and the lid sank into the can. He fished it out with his dirty fingers and handed the beans to his uncle. "Sorry," he said sheepishly.

"Just a touch of mountain seasoning." Dillon set the can between some glowing coals.

After dinner, the two sat around the dying embers

of the campfire. Dillon poured them each a cup of mountain mud.

Cordell sipped from his steaming mug and wrinkled his nose. "I've never had coffee before," he confessed, then tried another sip. "I wonder what Mom would say if she knew."

They sat listening to the breeze whooshing softly through the treetops.

"You think we'll find Dad?"

"Sure we will."

Except for a half moon, blackness had swallowed the light. Dillon looked up, his eyes tracing the faintly glowing skyline. For a long moment, his heart was overwhelmed at the vastness of the mountains. He tried to push his worried thoughts away, but they lodged in the pit of his stomach like a bad meal. Deep inside, Dillon was not as confident as he sounded.

CHAPTER 10

His ashes in a peaceful urn shall rest;
His name a great example stands, to show
How strangely high endeavours may be blest,
Where piety and valour jointly go
John Dryden

Maine
Wednesday, June 21

It looked to Anna as if half the residents of the tiny village of Port Williwaught had turned out for Malcolm O'Neil's funeral. She knew it wasn't because he was a nationally known syndicated columnist, but simply a well-liked native son.

As Anna drove down the town's main street, people emerged from kiln-like houses and shiplap cottages. They wore their Sunday best as they trudged down maple-lined streets to say good-bye to their friend and neighbor.

Anna pulled up to the old church—the place of her

baptism. The historic building had stood unchanged by the passage of time, constant and comforting—like her father had been. Anna's eyes followed the round arches under which her parents had been married, and beyond, to the crypt where her mother's ashes were laid to rest. Anna had no recollection of her mother, who had died when she was a toddler, but Malcolm had done his best to keep the memories alive. Anna smiled, remembering how his face lit up with love whenever he spoke of her.

"They'll finally be together," she whispered.

Many of Malcolm's media colleagues had traveled from eastern cities to pay their final respects. They moved along with the procession of locals slowly trudging from the church to the crypt.

Anna held her head high as she walked, refusing to make a spectacle of her grief. But, she was distracted. Behind a wall of mourners, a vagrant bobbed up and down as if trying to catch a peak.

Anna tried to ignore the rude intrusion. She pulled the collar of her jacket around her neck and came to a stop beside the minister.

He offered a funeral benediction as the crypt was opened and Malcolm's urn was placed beside his wife's. Anna looked on, cold and numb, as the heavy slate door was sealed.

When the protocol ended, Anna found herself engulfed in a swarm of condolences. She felt trapped, but did her best to endure the gestures. "Thank you for coming. It means a lot," she repeated with a mounting sense of panic.

When Anna could take no more, she broke free. Uttering apologies, she hurried toward a narrow trail that led to a thickly wooded area.

Anna walked briskly, as if she could outpace her sorrow, moving on through the forest until the quiet sounds of nature soothed her pain. Just off the trail, at the confluence of two small creeks, Anna lowered herself to the ground beneath a massive oak tree and stared off into the woodlands. Except for the jet contrails that sliced across the sky overhead, and a discarded can bobbing in the stream, it would have been easy for Anna to imagine these woods as they might have been a hundred years ago. Yet the concept of time seemed irrelevant in her grief.

Anna closed her eyes, trying to recall the happiness she had felt only a week ago.

A twig snapped in the woods. She turned her head to see a man standing there. The vagrant from the funeral!

Anna jumped to her feet and studied him warily. Though partially hidden behind a bushy calico beard, his face twitched. With eyes riveted on Anna, he scratched his neck and tugged at the dingy collar of his wrinkled cotton shirt.

The stranger took a step closer. Anna tensed, trying to assess both his age and her ability to outrun him.

Under the dark ledges of full-bodied eyebrows, his eyes glowed with intensity. "Don't be scared, Anna. I just need to talk to you."

"Who are you?" She positioned herself defensively beside a tree.

"William Vonsetter. I used to know your father . . . knew him very well in fact. But, things happened."

Anna's eyes narrowed. "What happened?" The air shifted, transporting the acidic smell of his body odor.

The man wagged his head and stifled a cough. "Long time ago . . . Malcolm and I were friends." Vonsetter shrugged. "But he didn't listen to me. Nobody did." His eyes locked on Anna and his countenance lightened. "I spoke with Malcolm before he died. He was finally ready for the truth." A look of satisfaction flashed across his ruddy features. "He believed me!"

Before he died? Anna thought with mounting tension. "What did Malcolm believe?" she asked, feeling her throat tighten.

"People are being deceived. Global warming, greenhouse gases. All misleading data." William's disjointed words pulsed rapidly. "It's gone too far. Political capital. Millions of dollars. Don't you see? It all fits." His eyes flicked nervously up and down the trail. "I can't stay." He turned away.

"Mr. Vonsetter—William, was it?"

He hesitated.

"How can I reach you? I mean, if I have any questions."

"You don't believe me. Probably think I'm crazy."

His shoulders slumped, and the excitement in his voice was gone. "Find the truth," he admonished. "Open your eyes. I'll be in touch." He hurried down the trail and disappeared from sight.

Truth? Anna wondered what that word meant to an obviously unbalanced old man.

—⁓—

Wednesday, June 21

The telephone rang on the investigator's desk. Anna paused so Corpizio could answer.

He let it ring. "Go on."

"The man just showed up at my father's funeral," Anna O'Neil said with a shudder. "He gave me the creeps."

"What was his name again?" the investigator asked. He riffled through a stack of clutter on his desk and produced a notepad.

"William Vonsetter." Anna watched Investigator Corpizio jot down the information. "Do you think he might be a suspect?"

"It's worth checking into." Corpizio pushed himself up from the desk and crossed to the doorway, where he summoned one of Port Williwaught's officers. He handed him the note. "Could you call state headquarters and have 'em run this name? Oh, and one more thing," Corpizio said. "Where do you keep the coffee around here?"

"I never drink it. It's not healthy." The young officer grinned. "Besides, might make my trigger finger nervous."

"Coffee is a staple down at the state office—keeps us awake." Corpizio rolled his eyes at the officer. "And I had to draw a field case with a health nut."

Anger percolated in Anna's bosom and she flashed the investigator a searing look. "I'm sorry if my father's murder bores you." She slapped her palms on the desk and launched from her chair.

"Believe me, Ms. O'Neil, I want to find your father's killer just as much as you." Corpizio scratched the end of his long nose. "Tell you what—there's a diner across the street. I'll fill you in on the investigation over some lunch."

Anna's anger faded as the investigator politely held the door open and escorted her across the street.

At the diner, Anna ordered a cup of herb tea. The waitress set a cup of black coffee on their table, left, and returned a moment later with the tea.

An awkward silence filled the space between them.

"So you're a tree hugger?" he asked.

Over the rim of her teacup, Anna stared at Corpizio. "Your redneck is showing."

"You don't like me much, do you, Ms. O'Neill?"

"I don't dislike you," she said. "I guess I just resent

the reason for you being here."

"I understand." He slurped his coffee. "Mind if I try again? So, you're a game biologist. Sounds interesting. What made you choose that line of work?"

"Malcolm always had a profound respect for nature." Anna lowered her head and studied a wisp of steam curling from her tea. She looked up and sighed. "The truth is, I did something bad once—when I was a kid. I guess you could say I've been trying to make up for it ever since."

The investigator's eyebrow rose and Anna grew flustered. "It was nothing criminal," she quickly added.

Corpizio leaned forward, his hands clasped together. "Go on."

Anna scowled and shifted in her seat. "Is this how you get confessions?"

"I wish it was always this easy."

"All right, but I'm only telling you this so you won't let your imagination run wild." Anna set her cup down. "Malcolm had just punished me. I don't remember why. I only remember wanting to hurt him back. There was a nest of new eggs that he'd shown me a few days before." Anna lifted a spoon from the saucer and tapped it lightly on her teacup. "I broke the eggs." She set the spoon on the table, recalling how easy it had been to poke holes in the shells.

Anna straightened in her chair, wiped sweaty hands on her jeans, and looked the investigator in the eyes.

"When Malcolm found out what I did, he wept. It was the first and only time I ever saw my father cry." Goose bumps rose on Anna's arms and she took a drink of lukewarm tea.

"Children do childish things," Corpizio said.

Anna smiled. "Well, that childish thing has been the motivating force behind my desire to protect wildlife. But, enough about that. Have there been any new developments in my father's murder investigation?"

"The forensic team has wrapped things up," Corpizio said, "so you're free to go back to the island."

"But you don't have any idea who killed my father yet, do you?"

He shook his head. "We're in the process of piecing together events, but the forensic evidence is pretty weak. We've got the caliber of bullet, but no gun. We dusted for prints and came up with Malcolm's, yours, and one from a glass that's not on file. Was your father expecting any guests?"

"I don't know," Anna whispered. A brooding thundercloud shadowed her thoughts. Malcolm had always been a gracious host. Someone, it seemed, had not returned his kindness.

Anna turned the sapphire ring on her finger—her last birthday gift from Malcolm. "Did you ever find the rest of the note?"

"No," Corpizio said. "We looked everywhere."

The investigator motioned the waitress for a refill.

"We pulled the tape on the answering machine and would like you to listen to some voices, see if you recognize them."

"Yes, of course," she said. "What about motive?"

"As a columnist, your father probably made enemies. People with opinions often do. We're running leads." Corpizio set his mug down. "Do you happen to know what your father was working on?"

Anna shook her head. "It should be on his computer."

"Yeah, that's what we thought." Corpizio ran a finger over chapped lips. "Couldn't find a thing. We sent the hard drive to the lab to see if our boys can recover any deleted files." He fished some change out of his pocket and threw it on the table. "In the meantime, we're sifting through some of your father's papers. Every day the boys uncover a new stack."

Anna envisioned Malcolm sitting at his cluttered desk, peering over reams of paperwork. Her fleeting smile faded. "What if the killer didn't find what he was looking for?"

Corpizio's silence said it all.

CHAPTER 11

From the end of the earth I will cry to You,
When my heart is overwhelmed;
Lead me to the rock that is higher than I.
Psalm 61:2

Wyoming
Thursday, June 22

The phone rang in the middle of the night. Grace opened her eyes. *Reuben,* she thought with a mixture of hope and dread.

Milo tossed the quilt from his wiry frame and padded on bare feet to the kitchen. Grace followed, wrapping her robe around her shoulders.

With her heart thumping, Grace braced herself as her husband answered. News that came in the cusp of darkness was seldom good. "Please, God," she whispered.

"What? Say that again." Milo listened to the caller. "Yeah, I'll be right there." He hung up and hurried back to the bedroom. "Where are my overalls?"

"In the laundry," Grace said.

"Well, get 'em out. Pastor Charlie Wait's barn church is on fire."

Grace dug her husband's clothes from the hamper and watched Milo thrust skinny legs into his jeans and slip into an old pair of boots.

"The church?" she said, trying to process the information. "I can't believe it."

"Well, I don't have time to convince you." Milo grabbed the keys to the Subaru and headed for the door.

Grace thought about her youngest son, Dillon, who had just joined the volunteer fire department. He was in the mountains looking for Reuben, she recalled with relief. "Are backup units on the way?"

"I don't have time to yammer with you." He gave his wife a hasty peck on the cheek. "I'll be careful." Milo slammed out the door, leaving Grace with her worries.

CHAPTER 12

Trust to future, howe'er pleasant;
Let the dead Past bury its dead!
Act, act in the living Present!
Heart within, and God o'erhead!
Henry Wadsworth Longfellow

Maine
Thursday, June 22

A stiff breeze blew in from the ocean, but Anna refused to budge. She had sat on the deck all morning, staring out to sea, avoiding the inevitable task of sorting through Malcolm's things. Every item was a treasure, a memento of a precious life, a father's love. A stinging gust tousled her hair. She pulled her sweater tighter. The cold wind seemed fitting.

Someone called Anna's name. She leaned forward on the Adirondack chair and caught sight of Corpizio coming up over the rise from the boathouse, a brown paper sack in one arm. He spotted her and waved, the wind flapping at his jacket.

"You have something positive to tell me?" Anna called when he came within earshot.

Corpizio joined her on the deck. "We're working on it." His dark hair blew back, exposing a thinning crown. He smoothed it down with his free hand. "You think we can go inside?"

Anna slid from the chair and he followed her through the French doors to the kitchen. "Want some coffee?" she asked. "Stupid question." Without waiting for a response, she filled a mug, set it down in front of him, and joined him at the table. "What's in the bag?"

"Your father's answering machine." Corpizio opened the paper sack. "There were two tapes. One we found in the machine. The other we discovered in the back drawer of the entryway desk." He plugged the machine into a nearby outlet. "We've identified most of the callers, but there are a couple of voices we haven't been able to pinpoint."

Corpizio punched the playback button. A taut, manic voice issued from the speakers. "Malcolm. Need to see you. Tomorrow—in town. I'll find you."

Anna leaned forward. "That's Vonsetter!" She gripped the edge of the table so hard her knuckles turned white. "That lunatic killed my father!" Anna thrust herself from the table.

Corpizio leaned forward and raised a hand. "Calm down. Just because the guy called your dad doesn't necessarily make him a killer."

Anna bit on her lip, poked at the upturned corner of a rug with her toe and dropped back to her chair.

The investigator dumped a manila envelope on the table and plucked another cassette from its contents. "This is the one we found in the drawer. There's no telling how old it is but, if you wouldn't mind . . ." Without waiting for a reply, the investigator slipped the new tape into the machine and punched the button.

"Hello, Malcolm." The man's voice was smooth. "I'll be passing through in the next few days and I'd love to drop in. Maybe have a few beers, talk over old times. See you soon."

"The voice sounds familiar." Anna rubbed her forehead. "I don't know."

"We've got the original at the station. You can keep this copy. Something may come to you later." The investigator stood, but hesitated. "Just so you know— we're doing everything we can to find William Vonsetter."

—⁕—

Thursday, June 22

"A lifetime of work," Anna said as she turned another page of her father's scrapbook of newspaper columns. From the east coast to the west, millions of people had read Malcolm's opinions, but for Anna, that was little consolation. She turned more pages and scanned the titles.

"The Costly Price of Oil."

"Fresh Science at the Global Warming Summit."

"America's Shrinking Wilderness."

Malcolm had left his daughter more than an island—he had left a legacy. Anna's eyes filled with tears, for her father had also left an empty place in her heart.

Anna closed the scrapbook and placed it in a box to ship back to Wyoming. She finished the tedious work of sorting. Most things, Anna decided, would stay as they had been.

She stood, stretched, and checked the clock on the mantle. It was only 2:00 PM. The hours seemed to move as slowly as a New York traffic jam. Anna drummed her fingers on the desk, wondering when the phone would ring with the news she longed to hear: *"We've caught your father's killer."*

Anna grabbed her jacket and went outside. She walked briskly, with no particular direction in mind. The island air was crisp beneath a lavender sky, and the ocean whispered soothing sounds to Anna, but it was not enough to chase the shadows from her soul. She walked on, past sandy washes, over rocky beaches. With each turn, an old memory surfaced, followed by a fresh surge of grief.

Anna paused by the water's edge and stared blankly out to sea. A gale of salty wind blew hard against her shoulders. She braced herself stubbornly. *"You'd wrestle with the wind if given a chance,"* Malcolm used to say.

Her fingers absently traced the delicate chain around her neck and stopped at the charm it held: a golden shell with a single pearl mounted in its center. Malcolm had given it to her on her twelfth birthday. She closed her eyes, allowing recollections to float her back to that happy occasion.

"You're getting warmer, little Anna."

A barefoot, freckled tomboy, she moved with agile ease upon the jagged rocks.

Malcolm caught up with her in the hidden cove, but she hurried on ahead. "Oh, now you're getting really warm!"

Anna giggled and scaled the stone steps to the narrow cavern with ease.

"How did you know?" Malcolm exclaimed.

She perched on tiptoe, reached inside the hiding place, and produced a brightly wrapped gift. Anna threw her head back in delight. "Ha!"

"You're almost a young lady now," her father said as he fastened the necklace around her throat. "I guess I can't call you Little Anna anymore."

The implication of the memory began to sink in. Anna's fingers dropped away from the charm and her mind turned to the note Malcolm had left on the table. "Little Anna. He wrote 'Little Anna'!"

She took the shortest route to the hidden cove, covering the ground like a gazelle. Anna's heart thundered with anticipation as she neared her destination. Grateful that the tide was low, she stepped carefully over the rock outcropping, then dropped down to the sandy beach.

It had been years since Anna was there, but the hidden cove had remained unchanged. Wasting no time, she hurried to the cave and felt for the ledge. Her fingers touched something. She withdrew the envelope and stared at it in disbelief.

In the cleft of the rock, Anna knelt to read the contents. Malcolm's last words were scribbled on the piece of missing newsprint. "The Canaan Creed."

CHAPTER 13

*Be kindly affectionate to one another with brotherly love,
in honor giving preference to one another; not lagging in
diligence, fervent in spirit, serving the Lord; rejoicing in
hope, patient in tribulation, continuing steadfastly in
prayer; distributing to the needs of the saints,
given to hospitality.*
Romans 12:10-12

Wyoming
Thursday, June 22

Grace's old Subaru wagon rattled past the burnt-out remains of the barn church and continued up the road to a vintage mobile home.

She lifted the still-warm casserole from the seat beside her, climbed the rickety stairs, and knocked.

Pastor Charlie Waits looked happy to see her. "Come in," he said, holding the door open.

Grace held out the casserole, nestled in a warming quilt. "I brought you some lasagna."

Charlie accepted the gift and took a long, satisfied whiff. "You shouldn't have—but I'm glad you did!"

"Whenever I don't know what else to do, I cook." Grace rubbed her round stomach. "I guess that goes without saying."

Charlie smiled. "I am blessed to have such good friends."

Grace set the casserole dish on the counter. "I'm sorry about the fire."

The pastor offered Grace a chair and some coffee. "It was a shock," he said, settling down at the table. "Sometimes bad things happen, but in the end it all works out."

Grace recalled the trials of Charlie's past: years of alcoholism, desertion by his wife, even a brief stint in jail. Plenty of bad things had happened in his life. "Do you really believe that everything turns out okay?"

Pastor Waits looked surprised by the question. "The Bible says that everything works together for good if you love God." He grinned. "I love God, so . . ."

"I wish I could have such faith," Grace said with a wistful sigh.

"Reuben?" Charlie asked.

Grace's eyes brimmed with tears. "I've also been worried about Cordell. And now, Dillon is having a hard time making ends meet." She swirled her coffee and stared at the dark liquid.

"I know just what you need." Charlie reached for

his Bible, thumbed through its pages, and found what he was looking for. "Peace I give you—the peace that passes all understanding." Charlie closed the Book. "John 14:27 is a great Scripture to remember, especially when things get rough. God will hold us up if we'll let Him. All He asks us to do is believe."

The words soaked into Grace's heart like a spring rain on parched ground. She wiped a tear from the corner of her eye and her heart swelled with gratitude. "Good heavens, Pastor. I came here to encourage you."

Charlie smiled and took Grace's hand. "God will work things out."

Grace searched her old friend's face and found hope—even in a world where people burned churches.

—⁂—

Thursday, June 22

At the base of the mountain, Peter sat motionless, as though in a trance. He had been sitting there for hours. From this vantage point, he could see the Pristine Valley to the right and the town of Cedar Ridge to the left. His eyes lingered on the blackened spot that had once been a church. Soon, he would leave this place, but there was one thing left to do.

He stood and gazed up at the jutting mountain, as though trying to absorb its texture. He lifted his backpack and embarked on his quest.

Above him loomed a formidable granite cliff guarded by slippery talus slopes. Reaching the face proved the biggest challenge of all. Peter made countless runs for the cliff, only to slide down on the loose shale-like rocks. He felt as if the mountains were challenging his right to ascend. His blood pumped with adrenaline. Fueled by anger, he charged upward, finally making it to the rocky face. He clung to the cliff, resting for a moment against the granite. He pushed on again.

Peter continued his ascent, carefully testing each hold as he went. Midway up, his weary legs began trembling. The rocks felt slippery beneath his sweaty fingers. Fear gripped Peter. He closed his eyes and summoned more strength. *Don't look down,* he cautioned himself.

One more hold, and then another. Finally, a rock ledge came into view. Peter pushed his muscles until he collapsed in a heap on the cool slab. He pulled a water bottle from his pack to soothe his parched throat and allowed a gentle breeze to coax his tired frame. After a few moments' respite, Peter forced himself to go on, wondering if his Crow ancestors had had a similar experience.

With determination and renewed vigor, Peter continued his ascent. Swiftly, but carefully, he climbed pausing when his muscles began shaking from fatigue. He willed himself to move.

With scratched and bloody hands, Peter pulled his

weary body up onto the last ledge and stood. Euphoria bubbled from within and his heart thumped wildly in his chest. It was like a bittersweet homecoming without a family to embrace. Now, at least half of his reason for coming to Wyoming had been satisfied. The other he would count a loss. Rage swelled in his bosom. It didn't matter. The only thing that mattered was the high ground where he now stood—the edge of the world.

Peter knelt to scoop a handful of soil. His eyes fell on the faint outline of a boot print. He rose slowly and looked around, imagining phantom eyes staring at him. A sudden unease skittered across his flesh. But, when he looked again, a breeze had swept the imprint away. Before long, Peter convinced himself that the boot print had been merely a product of an overactive imagination.

The young man assembled his pup tent, on the plateau near the cliff's edge. Peter felt his way down an outcropping to a ledge where he settled back to watch the sunset. The Wyoming sky was aflame with brilliant pink and orange hues that spread across the western sky and slowly melted away. He sat on the overlook, barely moving. On the far horizon, the moon appeared as a brilliant gemstone set among a thousand diamond stars.

Peter fought to control his deep emotions. Beneath the sky, his anger melted away. For now, the frightening years of his childhood were behind him. Time passed slowly as the crimson sky faded to purple and then to black. He looked up at the canopy of twinkling stars.

There seemed to be nothing between Peter and the heavens.

Muscle fatigue set in. His legs throbbed, demanding Peter's attention. Under the night sky, he bouldered back up the plateau. Peter burrowed through the flap of his tent, fumbled in the dark for his flashlight, and switched it on. With a start, he realized the backpack had already been unzipped. Peter knew he had not left it that way. He did a quick inventory, but nothing was missing. *You're imagining things*, he told himself. Still, the possibilities unsettled him.

He climbed into his sleeping bag and lay as still as a corpse, listening hard for any sound that would convince him that he was not alone. After a while, even the winds began to seem sinister. All night, Peter lingered on the edge of sleep. By the time the morning sun rose, he had made the decision to leave.

Peter packed his things quickly, keeping a watchful eye on the rocks and brambles. Something moved! Spooked, the young Native American scrambled down the rocky ledge more quickly than he should have. One misstep later, Peter saw the world passing in a granite haze. Bloodied fingers clawed in vain to slow his descent. Peter hit the ground with a thud.

CHAPTER 14

So, when a raging fever burns,
We shift from side to side by turns;
And 'tis a poor relief we gain,
To change the place, but keep the pain.
                    Isaac Watts

Maine
Friday, June 23

Anna O'Neil marched into the sheriff's station and handed Investigator Corpizio the envelope she had found at the hidden cove. "I have no idea what this means," she insisted, "but I'm sure Malcolm meant for me to find this clue."

Corpizio read the paper and spoke the words aloud. "The Canaan Creed." He escorted Anna to his cramped office and invited her to sit.

She chose to stand.

"Think hard, Ms. O'Neil."

"I have!" Anna paced the room, raising her arms

and letting them drop in exasperation. "I couldn't sleep last night thinking about it!" She plopped down on an office chair and ran her fingers through her windblown hair. "I need to go home. I've got work to do in Wyoming. Besides, I'm afraid I'll go crazy if I stay here."

Corpizio propped his elbow on his desk and leaned forward, chin resting on his hands. "That might not be a bad idea. There's nothing you can do here anyway."

"What if something comes up?" Anna vacillated. "A new development?"

"I'll call."

Anna eyed the investigator suspiciously. "You're not trying to get rid of me, are you?"

The investigator looked down his hawkish nose. "You're the one who brought up the subject of leaving."

"Yes, but you agreed too fast." Anna folded her arms across her chest.

Corpizio's mouth curled into a wry smile. "You remind me of why I'm not married." He chuckled. "Look, Ms. O'Neil, we're on the same side."

"You're right. I'm sorry." Anna rose and moved toward the door. She stopped at the evidence table and plucked up a stack of papers. "What's this?"

The investigator joined Anna at the table. "A record of Malcolm's phone calls going back six months." He removed the papers from her hand and set them back where they belonged. "A couple of the calls were made from a phone booth. Could have been Vonsetter."

Corpizio's brow wrinkled. "What do you know about the Endangered Earth Alliance?"

"Why do you ask?"

"Your father made a few recent calls to them."

"They're an environmental group," she said. "Malcolm was very generous with certain nonprofit organizations. Maybe the Endangered Earth Alliance was one of them. I wouldn't be surprised—they're one of the best." Anna shrugged. "Or he may have been working on a column about them."

"Could be," Corpizio said. "He also made a couple of calls to the Maine Fish and Wildlife Service and the Environmental Protection Agency."

The door opened and Detective Dobbs walked in, holding a long sheet of paper. "This just came in." The young lawman's eyes stopped on Anna, and flicked back to Corpizio. "Sorry. I thought you were alone."

"It's okay. What do you have?"

The young detective handed the fax to his superior, but did not wait for him to read it. "Vonsetter was once a renowned physicist," he blurted. "I mean top-level stuff. After that, this guy just seemed to drop off the map. Lives a nomadic lifestyle."

"Sometimes those genius types crack," Corpizio suggested.

Detective Dobbs thumped the paper with his finger. "The man drives a lime-green Chevy truck with an old Travel Queen camper on the back."

"What connection does William Vonsetter have to my father?" Anna cut in.

Corpizio folded the fax and dropped it on the table. "If you'll excuse us, Ms. O'Neil, we have a lot of work to do."

"The last thing I want to do is keep you from finding my father's killer," Anna said as she headed for the door. Still, curiosity coiled its fingers around her thoughts.

CHAPTER 15

Years to a mother bring distress,
But do not make her love the less.
William Wordsworth

Wyoming
Friday, June 23

Grace braced herself for a whirlwind as Jody breezed through the door of the Fischer Creek Café with little Christy in tow.

"Grace, did you hear?" her daughter-in-law asked breathlessly. "They think the fire at the church was deliberately set. Poor Pastor Charlie. Who would do such a thing?"

"It's terrible," Grace agreed as Christy climbed into her lap. Grace kissed her granddaughter's soft cheek and looked patiently at the child's mother. "I took Pastor Charlie a casserole yesterday."

Jody leaned over the counter, eagerness sparkling in her eyes. "What did he say? Does he know who set the fire? Is he devastated?"

Grace finished filling a salt shaker and let Christy screw the cap on. "He said that everything will work out."

"How does he know that?"

"Because he loves God and . . ." Grace noticed the perplexed look on Jody's face. "Never mind, honey."

Jody grabbed a rag and worked over a spot of syrup on the counter. She looked up, squinted through the sunny window and exclaimed, "Dillon's back!"

Grace watched the truck and horse trailer rattle past the window toward the side parking lot.

When Dillon walked through the door, Grace eyed him eagerly, hoping for good news. Her heart sank with one look at her younger son's face.

"Sorry, Ma. No sign of Reuben. We followed some tracks to the ravine where they found Duke. About five miles from there, I found a broken piece of a lash rope, but that's all." Dillon kicked at the rug in a fit of frustration. "I wish I could have stayed up there longer, but I need to get some logs down to the mill or they'll cancel my contract."

Grace noticed dark circles under his eyes and offered a reassuring smile. "That's okay, Son. You tried."

"Hey, guess who I brought back?" Dillon tilted his head toward the door as Cordell walked in.

Christy hopped from her grandmother's lap as Grace stood and opened her arms to embrace her teenaged grandson. "Good heavens, you've brightened my day!" She held him tight, then reluctantly let go. "Honey, what's the word on your grandpa's condition?"

"Don't know. I've been on the mountain with Uncle Dillon. Hey, I could use a cup of coffee," he added in a matter-of-fact tone.

Trying not to look surprised, Grace filled a mug, set it down in front of Cordell, and offered him cream and sugar. "Your mother said it was okay for you to drink this?"

Cordell squared his shoulders. "I've made up mind. Things are gonna be different with me 'n Mom. In fact, I'm heading up to Kragler Pass tomorrow with Uncle Dillon. He's promised to teach me how to use a chainsaw and do some logging." Cordell sniffed. "Hey, do I smell chili?"

Soon the lunchroom crowd began to trickle in and Grace divided her time between duties and family. Jody pitched in, chattering away as she waited tables, while Milo worked the gas pumps and the cash register.

"It's busier than usual," Dillon commented as Grace cleared his empty bowl.

Milo grunted like a bear and rolled his eyes. "Yeah, we've been feedin' a whole crew. That high-flyin' billionaire brought in some fancy construction firm to build his log castle up on the mountain."

"I wonder if they're hiring," Dillon said.

"It wouldn't hurt to ask," Grace said, pouring another cup of coffee.

Milo pursed his lips and looked at his son as if he

had lost his mind. "You'd want to work for some LA bigwig?"

"I've got a family to feed, Dad." Dillon opened a package of crackers, slid one into his mouth, and chewed. "I've heard rumors about more access closures—Tumble Creek, to be exact. If that happens, I'll only have one area left for logging and I won't be able to meet my quota." Dillon's countenance darkened and he slipped into a brooding silence.

"Well, don't get your hopes up about getting a construction job. I hear that mansion is just about finished."

"Good heavens, Milo, don't be so negative," Grace scolded. She bent over and took little Christy's hand in hers. "You want to help grandma?"

In the kitchen, Grace supervised as the child stirred a wooden ladle around the big pot of chili.

"Grandma, what can I bring for show-and-tell tomorrow?" Christy asked. "Jimmy brought his new kitten, but Mom won't let me bring my goldfish."

"I'm sure you'll think of something."

"I made a picture for you. Wanna see it?"

Grace wiped her hands on her apron and waited patiently as Christy retrieved a paper from her pocket. The child carefully unfolded it and held it out to see.

"What a beautiful mountain!" Grace said with enthusiasm. "I see some deer." She took her time inspecting the primitive crayon drawing. "But there aren't any trees."

Christy poked out her lower lip and batted her eyes. "Cause Daddy killed 'em all," she cried. "That's why all the deer are so skinny."

Grace tried to hide her shock. "What do you mean, honey?"

"When Daddy cuts down trees, he kills them. That's what my teacher says."

Grace checked the order window and put some burgers on the grill, giving herself a few moments to gather her composure. She turned back to Christy. "I have an idea for show-and-tell," Grace said with a mischievous smile. "How about bringing Grandma?"

Christy clapped her hands and jumped up and down. "I'll be the only one to show a grandma!"

Grace stooped to kiss her granddaughter's cheek. "You make me so happy."

Christy patted her grandma's pudgy arm. "That's good, 'cause you haven't looked very happy since Uncle Reuben got lost."

The child was right, Grace thought. How could a mother be happy when one of her own was missing?

CHAPTER 16

Forests have ears, and fields have eyes;
Often treachery lurking lies . . .
Henry Wadsworth Longfellow

Wyoming
Friday, June 23

Reuben Fischer had felt safe on the plateau. Perched atop the steep cliff, nestled behind a wall of brush, he'd observed the government trackers as they systematically marched through grids of terrain. The shallow cave was an added bonus. The mass of rock was cool enough to fool infrared detectors, and by late afternoon, it had soaked in enough rays to keep him warm through the night. It had been the perfect place to hide until that young Native American kid showed up.

Reuben thought of the risk he had taken when the young man fell from the cliff, but he couldn't turn his back. With a shudder, Reuben recalled the sound of bone on bone as he straightened the femur and fashioned a makeshift splint. He had carried the unconscious kid three miles to the nearest road, spending his own precious energy in the process—energy he needed to conserve. Reuben hoped the kid would make it, but couldn't wait around to find out.

His stomach burned with hunger and his legs and back ached from fatigue, but he pushed those needs aside for those more pressing. In his haste to help the boy, Reuben had no doubt left behind signs—signs that an expert tracker could easily pick up. He needed to find a new place to hide.

Reuben recalled his first night on the run. He had waded downstream and scaled a granite wall with only a sliver of moonlight to illuminate his way. He would never forget clinging to the jagged overhang while the dogs closed in. Several times, his body had convulsed so violently he thought he might drop to his death. Somehow, he had made it. It was hard to believe that two weeks had gone by.

The sound of boots tramping on rocky soil shifted Reuben's mind back to the present. There was no time to waste. Selecting a large pine tree, he climbed, stopping only when the branches refused to support his weight. Hidden by thick boughs, Reuben waited and watched.

Moments later, he caught a glimpse of movement as the trackers passed beneath. The men had no dog with them to pick up his scent. That was a stroke of luck. Reuben stilled himself and prayed that no twig would break or pinecone drop to give away his hiding place.

The men walked on and Reuben breathed a silent sigh of relief. But he remained in place. Twenty minutes went by before the normal rhythms of the forest resumed. Squirrels chattered, birds chirped. Yet the soothing sounds of nature offered no consolation.

Reuben's thoughts turned to Duke. Had he survived? Worry dogged Reuben. A bead of sweat trickled down his whiskered face. When he wiped it away, the salty fluid stung his hand. In the dimming light, he studied his shredded skin and tried to think of the next step.

The best chance, he reasoned, would come with nightfall. Under the blanket of darkness, he could cover some ground. Reuben had no idea where he would go. Pushing aside thoughts of infrared detectors and night-vision glasses, he resolved to find a new hiding place before the first morning light.

As Reuben climbed down from the tree, his mind turned to his wife and son. He smiled at a memory retrieved from a sweeter time. Some days it had been hard to recall that they had once been happy. Reuben wondered if it could ever be like that again. Deep inside he knew that the chance of any reunion, let alone a happy one, would take a miracle.

—⚉—

Friday, June 23

Peter's tongue felt swollen and cardboard dry. He

tried to recall what had happened. The memory came in a fog. He had fallen from the mountain and now he was lying near the valley roadside. How he had gotten there was a mystery. The cliff was at least a mile away.

Peter lifted his hand and stared at his bent and bloodied fingers as if they were foreign objects. He tried to sit up, but grimaced as an excruciating pain shot through his right femur. Slowly Peter pushed his torso up with his elbows and looked at his leg. Someone had cut away his jeans and fashioned a makeshift splint. Beneath it, his thigh was purple and swollen.

Peter's head swam with pain. For a brief moment, he thought he was going to be sick. On the ground next to him sat his backpack. Peter found his water bottle and guzzled from it. He fell back in utter exhaustion.

Off in the distance Peter heard the sound of a car. Bracing himself against the pain, he raised his upper body. He spotted the blacktop, maybe fifteen yards away. Using his one good leg, he pushed himself toward the road. Each movement was excruciating. The meadow grass felt like cactus barbs on his shredded fingers.

The car came closer and Peter summoned strength to flag down the driver. He pushed his body up and lifted his arm. He could see it now—a blue sedan with out-of-state plates.

Peter swung his arm and yelled, but the car blew past. He curled his fist in anger and stifled a scream.

From around the bend another vehicle rolled into view.

Light danced before Peter's eyes and he lifted a weak arm in the air. Brakes squealed, balding tires crunched to a stop beside the road, and Peter collapsed in relief.

CHAPTER 17

It is no less true in this human kingdom of knowledge,
Than in God's kingdom of heaven,
that no man shall enter into it,
"except he become first as a little child."
Lord Francis Bacon

Wyoming
Monday, June 26

"I brought my Grandma Fischer for show-and-tell," Christy announced.

Grace beamed with pride as her little granddaughter led her to the front of the summer-school class.

The child wiped her runny nose. "Sometimes Grandma reads to me. And she lets me plant petunias with her. And she bakes yummy cinnamon rolls." Christy's face lit up. "And she's the softest grandma I know!"

A couple of the other children giggled.

"That's very interesting." From behind her desk,

the teacher stood. "Class, show-and-tell is over for today. It's time to work on your ABC project." Little desks opened in unison as the children withdrew their workbooks.

The teacher approached Grace and held out her hand. "It was good of you to come. It means so much to the children when family is supportive."

"I've had such fun!" Grace smiled at Christy, sitting at her desk with a fat pencil in her hand.

The teacher nudged Grace toward the door.

"If you don't mind, Ms. Sidell," Grace said, "I'd like to sit in on the class. It seems like the perfect opportunity to be supportive."

"Well," the teacher stammered, "I don't really encourage extended visits. They can be a distraction." The woman flashed an insincere smile.

"I promise to sit quietly in the back of the class," Grace pressed. "But if there's something you want me to do?"

With the same smile frozen on her face, the teacher declined Grace's offer to help, but directed her to a chair in the back of the classroom. "Now, if you'll excuse me," she said, "I need to instruct the children."

Grace watched Ms. Sidell move to the front of the classroom and write on the whiteboard.

"'A' is for what?" The teacher held her hand to her ear.

"Apple!" the students yelled.

Grace observed the teacher's expressive mannerisms and exaggerated enunciations. the slender woman encouraged the students to participate by encouraging them to use their imaginations.

The children read aloud, punctuating each sentence with an action. "Tommy ate the apple." They plucked an imaginary apple from a tree and pretended to eat. "Suzie kicked the ball." They kicked into the air and the room erupted in delighted giggles.

The children obviously liked their teacher. Grace wanted to like her too. It was possible that Christy was mistaken. Maybe Ms. Sidell had not really called Dillon a tree killer.

The morning grammar lesson wore on and the teacher's cool gaze flicked past Grace. The glance seemed pointed and cold.

By ten thirty, the classroom tempo increased with a lively round of math games, followed by recess. On the playground, Grace earned the title of "Bestest swing pusher and merry-go-round spinner ever!"

Ms. Sidell appeared on the steps and blew a whistle. "Recess is over!" she announced.

"Goodness, where has the morning gone?" Grace said cheerfully, joining the teacher. "The kids seem to be enjoying my visit."

The corners of Ms. Sidell's lips curled upward. "I'm sure."

Grace detected a hint of condescension in the teacher's tone.

"Single file," the teacher called. She waited for her class to obey. "I have a special treat for you, but you must be on your best behavior." Like Mother Goose, Ms. Sidell led the gaggle back to their little desks. "We're going to watch a movie." The woman punched the play button on her DVD and flicked the light switch off.

In the dim room, Grace located her seat in the back of the classroom.

The video portrayed a panoramic scene of mountains, majestic rocks, and tundra. The focus zoomed in on a lush green valley, where a litter of adorable pups frolicked in the tall meadow grass.

"The gray wolf," the narrator's resonant voice boomed. "Regal, loving, playful, and misunderstood."

The tranquil scene was shattered by the sound of gunfire. The pups scattered in terror. The camera turned to a gap-toothed mountain man. Animal hides were flung across the back of his mule—furry remnants of his victims. He raised his rifle and fired again. The mother wolf yelped in pain and fell to the ground while her frightened pups looked on.

"In ignorance and fear, man has destroyed these beautiful creatures. It's time to speak up."

The film rolled with feel-good footage of the gray wolf, from adorable pups to endearing alpha females.

Grace could not believe what she was seeing—a propaganda film for the reintroduction of the wolf. She looked at the tiny audience, barely out of diapers and hardly equipped to assess this politically charged issue. Impressionable thoughts were being manipulated!

As the film credits rolled, the teacher flipped on the light. "Now we have a really special treat." Ms. Sidell opened the door, and a silver-haired man walked in, carrying a wolf pup. High-pitched squeals of delight issued from the children. "Everyone, say hello to Mr. Addison Lee and his friend Shadow."

Addison Lee walked a circle around the room, holding the fluffy gray pup amid oohs, aahs, and wide-eyed interest.

"Can I pet him?"

"No, let me!"

"I said first!"

"I'm sorry, but I can't allow anyone to touch Shadow," Addison said. "He is an extremely timid animal."

Their four-footed guest enthralled the children. By the time Addison left, the whole class was convinced these wild animals were as tame as a Newfoundland puppy.

The teacher stepped forward. "Did everyone like Shadow?"

An emphatic chorus of "Yes!" exploded from the students.

"Raise your hand if you would like to help the wolves." Soft pink hands shot upward and wiggled enthusiastically. "Wonderful!" The teacher passed out Xerox copies of a letter.

Grace leaned over her granddaughter's desk and

followed along as Ms. Sidell read. "Dear Senators, please help bring the wolves back to their home." She paused. "Does everyone agree with this letter?"

A resounding "Yes" filled the room.

The teacher instructed her class to take out their color crayons. "I want you to draw pretty pictures of a happy wolf, living in the mountains," she said. "Last, I want you to sign your name with your pencils."

The children went to work, scribbling stick-figure dogs with big-toothy smiles. The pictures were punctuated with rolling hills, flowers, and sunny skies.

When Christy was done with her artwork, she retrieved her fat pencil. With tongue poking out in concentration, she printed her name on the letter. Grace's heart sank. This woman was using her classroom as a brigade of tiny lobbyists!

"I'll make sure these letters are sent to people who can help the wolves." Ms. Sidell said as she collected the papers.

When the last bell of the day rang, Grace gathered her thoughts and her courage. She lingered in the back until the last child had left the room. "Do you have a few minutes?" she asked the teacher.

Ms. Sidell's eyes shifted to her oversized wristwatch, then back to Grace. "I have a staff meeting to attend."

"I'll get right to the point. I've been surprised by some of the ideas Christy has been sharing with me. I had hoped it was a simple misunderstanding. But after the film and especially the letters . . ."

"If Christy's parents had any concerns, I'm sure they would have expressed them by now," Ms. Sidell interrupted. "After all, it is the last week of school before summer break."

Grace would not be put off. "Did you tell Christy that her dad was a tree killer? Dillon is a responsible logger who only cuts diseased and overcrowded trees. Did you know that thinning cuts actually make a forest healthier?"

Ms. Sidell raised her eyebrows. "I apologize if I've caused stress in your household, but it's my duty as a teacher to present the facts."

"Like that wolf movie you showed in class? There's another side to this issue."

"Science is on my side." The teacher strutted to her desk, where she gathered a stack of papers. "Now, if you'll excuse me."

Ms. Sidell slipped through the door, leaving Grace with a deep sense of frustration. It had not been her intention to make an enemy of Christy's teacher. She had only wanted to reason with her, adult to adult. So much for that idea.

CHAPTER 18

Tis better far to love and be poor, than be rich with an empty heart.
Sir Lewis Morris

Wyoming
Monday, June 26

Lily Harrington kept an eye on her husband as the private jet banked over the Wyoming mountains, then circled back to the Cedar Ridge airport for a flawless landing. Randolph pressed his face against the cabin window like a little boy.

"I feel exhilarated, Wildflower," Randolph said. "Wyoming is going to be my sanctuary. Here, the healing arms of Mother Nature shall embrace me. She won't let me down."

Lily was not so sure. She had been with Randolph in the evening hours, when exhaustion came to call, and she had lain beside her husband in the night as he thrashed about on sweat-soaked sheets. Leukemia was a tenacious foe.

As the jet taxied to a private hanger, Randolph turned and squeezed Lily's hand. She felt him tremble.

"Did you remember to take your medicine?" she asked.

Randolph drew his hand away. His eyes narrowed. "In the basement of our new home is a fully equipped clinic. There I will receive state-of-the-art treatments by a highly trained medical staff. That is all you need to know." Randolph's dark eyes held Lily firm. "My illness must never be mentioned. Do I make myself clear?"

Lily retreated to silence as the jet's cabin door opened. Randolph stood and offered his arm. "Our new life awaits."

In the modest Wyoming airport, a small gathering of environmentalists stepped forward to greet the couple.

"Welcome to Cedar Ridge." A silver-haired man offered his hand. "My name is Addison Lee. I'm the founder of the Pristine Valley Nature Coalition. It's a pleasure to meet you both."

"You're one of Anna O'Neil's mentors," Randolph said, offering a handshake. "I assume we will be working closely together on the upcoming wilderness dedication." Randolph summoned his chauffer with a snap of his fingers. He turned again to Addison Lee. "If you'll excuse us, we must get settled in."

As soon as the Harringtons' luggage was loaded into the back of the new Cadillac Escalade, they were on their way through the sleepy little town of Cedar Ridge.

Main Street housed an eclectic mixture of businesses, from retro-looking hardware stores to chic dress shops. Lily made a mental note of some shopping opportunities to explore.

"Quaint, don't you agree?" Randolph pointed ahead. "Do you see that canyon? Our valley lies just beyond." He brushed a loose strand of hair from Lily's cheek. "We'll be happy here."

Lily grasped her husband's words with a fist of hope. *Let it be true. Please let it be true.* It was a familiar mantra—one she had repeated as a child when shuffled from one foster home to another. Happiness had always seemed just out of reach.

"It's so pretty," Lily said, as they emerged from the canyon and a majestic vista blossomed before their eyes. In the Pristine Valley, the river spread wide and generous before an alpine field. Vibrant patches of sunlight outlined the shade of towering peaks. "It's one of the prettiest places I've ever seen. And the colors . . ."

"That's called alpine glow." Randolph smiled as the driver pointed the Cadillac up the paved road. "I believe these mountains will be my healing balm. My Shangri-La."

"I hope you're right." Lily said, pondering her own undefined beliefs. Nature seemed impersonal and God seemed far away.

"There it is, above the pines and aspens."

Lily followed the line of her husband's finger.

Through a tree break, she spotted the mansion—its multi-level roofline, competing with the mountains beyond. "It looks like a log castle."

Randolph seemed pleased with his wife's assessment. He postured himself like royalty.

The driver followed the road, which snaked along the edge of a willow-lined stream. Near the top, the view unfolded to an alpine meadow edged with aspen trees.

Lily's gaze rose to the towering cathedral windows. In their reflection, lazy clouds floated in an azure sky.

Randolph leaned forward and perched for a hasty exit as the driver rolled up to a substantial front porch. "It's stunning, don't you think?"

"It's certainly . . . large." Lily shot her husband a sideways glance as they climbed from the SUV. He paid no attention to her awkward choice of words.

Massive ironclad doors opened to a line of eager staff. "Mr. and Mrs. Harrington." The head butler stepped forward. "We have been expecting you."

Lily extended her hand to the man, but Randolph took her by the shoulder and ushered her across the threshold. "Introductions can wait, Wildflower." He escorted his bride into the cavernous room and swept his arms skyward where the river-rock hearth rose up to meet ample blond timbers.

She stared at the gigantic fireplace—big enough to stand in.

"I spared no expense with the furnishings—original Molesworth, not some imitation." Randolph smiled at Lily. "I suppose you'd like to see the kitchen. Women always do."

A middle-aged maid in a pressed black-and-white uniform led the way to the heart of the house.

The kitchen has been equipped with all commercial-grade appliances. Copper pots hung over green Italian marble countertops.

Lily stared at a domed solarium filled with plants. "Is that a little greenhouse?"

Randolph reached out and squeezed Lily's hand. "I knew you would enjoy this added touch. Nothing like the fragrance of fresh herbs, don't you think?"

Just off the kitchen, they walked into a vast dining room. A sprawling granite table, long enough to seat a small army sat in the middle surrounded by floor-to-ceiling windows. Outside, Lily spotted a lone deer as it grazed among the aspen trees.

"I am pleased, very pleased!" Randolph announced. "Here, nature herself is invited to dine with us."

The room felt cold to Lily. She nodded, but offered no comment. *Another detail, planned and executed by Randolph.*

Randolph put his hand on his wife's shoulder. "Come along, Wildflower. There is so much more to see."

Next stop was the library constructed to house

Randolph's prized collection of rare books. The room seemed oddly out of place in a mansion built to house vast spaces of light and air. The inlaid floor and wainscot was made of richly textured woods, set off by black towering built-in bookshelves. Randolph lingered long in this room, touching books and scrutinizing the workmanship of the shelves. "I'll let you in on a little secret indulgence of mine," he said, "I had mahogany flown in from Brazil. It was not an easy undertaking—especially since big-leaf mahogany is an endangered hardwood."

Lily lowered herself onto a supple leather couch while Randolph inspected the ladders that serviced the library. She watched with amusement as her husband rolled them back and forth, looking for flaws.

Finally satisfied, he turned and extended his arms toward a fully stocked wet-bar. "Would you care for a drink, Wildflower?"

Lily shook her head.

"Let's carry on, shall we?" Randolph prattled on as they climbed the grand staircase. "We'll save the basement for last, though I can hardly wait to see the movie theatre and gymnasium. You'll fall in love with the indoor swimming pool," he added, as they reached the upstairs landing. Randolph paused to catch his breath.

Lily squeezed his hand. "Are you alright?"

His lips pursed, "Of course. I'm fine!" he said tersely. "Don't let the stairs intimidate you, Wildflower. Just off the master bedroom you'll find a private elevator."

Lily glanced over her shoulder at the cavernous space below. The house was large enough to hold a small circus. She felt dizzy as Randolph took her by the hand and led her down a long corridor, past a small den and some furnished guest rooms.

When they arrived in the master bedroom, Lily's face ached from smiling.

"Have a look around while I test the fireplace," Randolph said.

A white eider-down comforter against blond wood walls did little to instill a feeling of warmth. Lily kept the thought to herself. "Wow—what a sight!" she said, pointing to the three large windows that came together for a panoramic view of the mountain.

"If you like this, you will adore the observation tower. With the aid of a telescope, you can see forever."

Lily followed her husband into the huge master bath to join his admiration of the sauna and Jacuzzi.

"I've had heated tile floors installed." He smiled. "It wouldn't be proper to have a bride with cold feet." Randolph reached behind a rock ledge and turned a valve and a waterfall tumbled over a series of flat rocks and flowed into a contoured basin. "Just like a natural mineral spring." Randolph turned aglow with satisfaction. "What do you think of it all?"

"I think . . . It's like standing on top of the world," she said, wondering why she felt so empty.

CHAPTER 19

Revocate animos—recall your courage!
Latin—Virgil

Maine
Monday, June 26

The sun had already set by the time Anna pulled up to the dock at Canaan Island. She knew it was never a good idea to travel after dark on the chilly waters off Maine's coast, but she justified the risk by telling herself that her time spent in town had been productive. The box of family mementos was at the post office and Anna had accessed the Internet at the Williwaught Library to purchase her airline ticket home.

As she secured the boat, her mind was full of last-minute details: clean cupboards, strip bedding, check locks and windows, and winterize the house.

There was no telling when she would find a reason to return.

Beneath a twinkling host of stars, Anna turned up

the collar of her jacket and trudged up to the house. It was time to say good-bye. Tomorrow, she would fly away and try to put the pieces of her life back together.

Anna unlocked the door to the house, wishing she were already in Wyoming. Another night alone on the island was almost more than her heart could take. Every room held a reminder of her loss.

In the kitchen, Anna searched the cupboards and refrigerator for perishables, finding just a few staples. The milk had gone sour. She dumped it down the sink and tossed the carton in the garbage can, along with the rest of the food items. She unplugged the fridge. *One down.* Anna scratched it off her list of things to do and started for the living room.

She stopped. Uneasiness crawled across her flesh, putting her senses on full alert. Anna had felt this way once before—in the mountains, when a grizzly was stalking her. She convinced herself that it was just her imagination, yet the feeling followed her from room to room. Little unsettling noises turned to sinister whisperings.

Anna busied herself stripping beds. Calmer now, she carried an armload of sheets to the laundry room and dropped them in the washer.

Something in the house crashed. Anna's throat constricted. She slipped her cell phone from her pocket and dialed Investigator Corpizio's number. He answered on the third ring.

"I need help," she whispered. "Someone is in the house."

"Stay on the line," Corpizio said.

She heard nothing but silence on the other end. After what seemed like an eternity, Anna picked up the jumbled sound of conversation. Corpizio finally came back on the line.

"Detective Dobbs lives a few minutes away. He's heading out now."

"Tell him to hurry," she said.

"I'm on my way too," Corpizio assured her.

The cell phone hissed with static as the connection began to break up.

"Corpizio?"

The line went dead.

Anna cautiously opened the laundry room door and peered down the hallway. Summoning her courage, she tiptoed around the corner to the living room and froze at as two loud bangs, like pots clattering together, issued from the kitchen. A faint scratching followed. Someone was definitely in the kitchen!

Anna lifted an umbrella from the stand near the door and crept closer, her heart pounding. Her breathing quickened. Instinct told her to run and hide, but something more powerful motivated her—justice for her father. Anna summoned the same courage that had carried her through the untamed wilderness of Wyoming. If Malcolm's killer was in the next room, he would have to confront a woman who had faced down wild animals.

Anna lifted her hand to the door. It creaked and she froze. A trilling noise issued from the kitchen. It was a familiar sound. Anna pushed open the door and swept her gaze through the room. A trashcan lay on its side, garbage strewn all over the floor.

The can moved. Anna stepped closer and touched it with the toe of her hiking boot.

A raccoon exploded from the garbage can and scurried under the kitchen table.

Blood thundered through Anna temples. *I don't know who scared whom the most.* She laughed.

The raccoon plumped defensively and trilled again.

"Hey, little guy." She patted her chest to calm her nerves. "You've caused a lot of trouble here tonight."

Corpizio!

Anna dialed his cell phone number again. "I'm sorry," a recorded voice said, "the subscriber you are trying to reach is unavailable." She tried once more, then gave up. Anna pushed open the kitchen door and gently shooed the raccoon back outside.

By the time Corpizio arrived, Anna had cleared up most of the mess.

"I'm sorry you had to come out here," she said.

"Best-case scenario," Corpizio said with a good-natured smile. "I assume Detective Dobbs did a quick check before he left?"

Anna frowned. "He never showed up."

Corpizio radioed the station, but received no

answer. "Something probably came up." His dark eyes scanned the room. "As long as I'm here, I might as well make sure the place is secure."

Anna followed the investigator through the house, checking windows and locks. In an unused guest room, they found a French door ajar.

"So that's how the raccoon got in," Anna said.

Corpizio looked somberly at her. "But who opened the door?" He pointed to a broken pane of glass beside the lock. "I don't know of many animals that could do that."

A chill blew through Anna's soul. "What are you saying?"

"Maybe you had more than one intruder here tonight."

CHAPTER 20

Dissensions like small streams are first begun;
Scarce seen they rise, but gather as they run.
Sir Samuel Garth

Wyoming
Tuesday, June 27

In the kitchen of the Fischer Creek Café, Grace plunged dirty dishes into the sudsy sink. "I think that poor woman really believes those things she's teaching the kids."

"Ought to be run out of town," Milo snapped. "That teacher is a troublemaker if ya ask me."

Grace immediately regretted telling her husband about her experience at Christy's summer school. Milo was even more agitated than normal. "Was the café busy this morning, dear?" she asked, trying to change the subject.

Milo mumbled something under his breath and stomped off toward the storage room.

"Hey!" someone hollered from the dining room. "This would be a great place for a restaurant!"

Grace recognized the nasal twang as that of one of the Badland boys. "Oh, no," she mumbled and peered through the order-window opening as the local misfits filed into the café. The tall leader, Juke, was followed by a little hedgehog of a fellow. A third man trailed behind, mute and pale as a ghost.

Juke tossed his greasy plaid Scotch-cap on the table as Grace emerged from the kitchen. "'Bout time," he smirked.

"You want menus?" she asked.

"Nope, just coffee."

The smell of sweat trailed from the door to the table where they sprawled. Grace grabbed the coffeepot, wishing it was a can of Lysol, and headed their way.

Juke snatched the cup as soon as Grace poured it. He took a long, loud slurp. "This ain't even hot," he complained. The other two sampled theirs and bobbed their heads in agreement.

"Milo around?" Juke slid a toothpick from the front pocket of his dingy shirt and slid it between cracked lips.

"I'm not sure where he is." It wasn't really a lie, Grace rationalized. For all she knew, Milo may have left the storage room.

Just then her husband clomped up the stairs from the cellar, his arms loaded with restaurant staples. "We're running low on tomatoes. Better put them on the reorder list."

Grace cringed. *Please Lord, don't let the Badland boys get Milo all worked up.*

"Hey, Fischer, you seen any of them government men creepin' around?" Juke asked.

"You mean the group of back-country rangers from the branch office?" Milo wiped a bead of sweat from his shiny scalp.

"Naw, those boys is small fry." He lowered his voice and glanced around. "Word has it they brought in a new team of trackers to hunt down that boy of yours. Came with all kinds of high-powered tracking equipment. All's I can say is, Reuben must be makin' 'em mighty nervous."

The little hedgehog of a man opened his mouth-hole and snickered. He held up his mug and flicked a glance in Grace's direction. "Gimme another shot of joe."

She ignored him.

"Hey, Milo, can you get yer woman's attention? I want a warm-up."

Grace gripped the coffeepot, wishing she had the courage to give Juke a warm-up he would not soon forget. *Be nice,* she told herself as she poured.

Nobody in town seemed to know from under which rock the Badland boys had slithered. The divisive trio had just shown up one day, spouting paranoid delusions and leaving behind a trail of fear and suspicion.

"For what it's worth," Juke cajoled, "I don't think Reuben killed that ol' rancher. I believe the government did that boy in." His tongue flipped the splintered toothpick to the other side of his mouth.

Grace froze in her tracks. "What did you say?"

The man studied Grace with dull eyes. "Duke Bassett died this morning." He took another slurp of coffee. "There's a lot of buzz around the hospital. The ol' boy's death was purdy sudden if you know what I mean." He drew in a breath and scratched a spotty outbreak on his cheek. "I heard that rancher was startin' to wake up. I figure somebody didn't want him talking."

The hedgehog rubbed his round stomach. "You know, I'm getting kinda hungry." His companions nodded. "Couple of menus," he demanded.

Grace looked at Milo in stunned silence. If what this man said was true, Reuben had just become a murder suspect.

CHAPTER 21

How strange it seems, with so much gone
Of life and love, to still live on!
John Greenleaf Whittier

Wyoming
Wednesday, June 28

Anna slipped into her hometown without any fanfare, just as she had hoped. Only the postal worker seemed to recognize her as she collected a bundle of mail. "How are you, Ms. O'Neil?"

"Tired," Anna said. *Broken*, she thought. "I mailed myself a package from Maine. Has it arrived yet?"

"This it?" He held up a padded manila envelope and inspected it. "It's got a Maine postmark."

"No, it was a box of mementos."

The postal worker gave her a bin to carry the mail—some looked like condolence cards. Anna sighed, tossed the bundle in the trunk of her car and headed for the comforts of home.

Outside Cedar Ridge, Anna turned onto County Road 41 and maneuvered skillfully over an obstacle course of deep ruts and potholes.

When the Cutter Creek Bridge came into view, Anna turned down a primitive dirt road. It had been days since a smile had graced her lips. Now her heart skipped with excitement as she followed the meandering curves of Cutter Creek, a sparkling path leading toward home. Just around the bend was the Crumbwalters' rickety old farm, and just three quarters of a mile beyond that Anna's refuge waited.

She spotted her modest log cabin, partially hidden from view by a patch of willows and quaking aspens. At the end of a narrow driveway, the Jeep slid to a quick stop. Anna threw open her car door as if she were a racehorse bursting from a stall. She smelled rosehips in full bloom, and the faint aroma of pine carried to the lowlands on a mountain breeze.

The first priority was an ice-cold drink from the glacier-fed creek. Anna hurried around the side of the cabin and down a short footpath. Beside the gurgling water, she sank to her knees, cupped her hands, and submerged them in the frigid water. Anna drank until she could drink no more. Satisfied, she drifted peacefully to her cabin.

Inside, the first thing Anna did was throw open the curtains and windows, allowing fresh air to pour into the living room. Sunlight fell upon the rich log walls and the cozy rock fireplace.

Anna drew comfort from familiarity: the tree-moss bark that hung above the entryway; a felled aspen tree wedged tightly between the floor and ceiling, which looked as if it had grown there; bundles of dried flowers hanging from the ceiling; pieces of petrified wood and quartz. Each item came with a tale of adventure.

Anna collapsed on her driftwood couch and made a mental list of things to do: unpack, check the answering machine, and fix lunch. It took all the effort Anna could muster to rise from the couch and move to the kitchen.

She foraged in her pantry for something to eat, found some Ramen noodles, and put the flames on under a pan of water.

She had just settled down to eat when the phone rang. She lifted the receiver on the third ring, but the caller had already hung up—*probably a telemarketer*. Anna replaced the receiver and checked the machine. There were no messages, yet the caller ID log was full. *Strange.*

Anna scrolled down the log. Public phone . . . public phone . . . public phone. All the same. She rubbed her arms—probably just some idealistic college student who admired her work.

Anna finished her lunch, trying to set her mind on everyday things. It was useless. All she could think about was what Investigator Corpizio was doing. Was he any closer to finding her father's killer?

—✺—

Maine
Wednesday, June 28

Investigator Corpizio stood on the mainland shore across from Canaan Island. In the frigid water, a diver bubbled to the surface with a body in tow.

Detective Dobbs's abandoned sedan had been located a few days earlier down the road from the Canaan Island dock. After someone discovered boot prints in mud beside the pier, divers were called in.

The diver hoisted the corpse to the sodden edge of the water. With a heavy heart Corpizio stepped forward to take a look. The body was bloated, face twisted in a grimace, eyes rolled back. It barely resembled Corpizio's friend. Gunshot to the head, a cursory glance told him. Death was swift. It was small consolation.

Behind him, the coroner's station wagon crunched to a stop on the gravel road as Corpizio tried to wrap his mind around the whole thing. The same person had now killed twice and one thing had become crystal clear: It was personal now.

Corpizio recalled the last time he had spoken with the detective. It was on the night Anna O'Neil had called about an intruder. Dobbs must have surprised the assailant as the killer fled Canaan Island.

A marked car bounced down the road toward the crime scene. A field officer stomped on his brakes and hopped from the idling cruiser. "We found a potential witness," he said, waving a report in his hand. "Little old lady who lives up the road. On the night in question, she saw a truck with a camper on the back."

Corpizio pinched the bridge of his nose. "Green, by any chance?"

"How'd you know? Ugly lime color, as the old lady put it."

Corpizio strode to his car, riffled through the glove box, and produced his notebook. He flipped through pages until he found what he was looking for.

Scribbled in haste, next to the name Vonsetter, was a description of his vehicle: a lime green truck with a camper on the back.

Corpizio snatched up the radiophone. "Put out an APB on William Vonsetter," he told the dispatcher. He braced himself for a long night back at the office.

—⋙—

Wyoming
Thursday, June 29

On her porch, Anna found the anticipated package. She retrieved it and raced back inside her cabin to open it. Anna reminisced as she unpacked Malcolm's leather-bound collection of literary classics, the bolo tie her father always wore, his pocket watch, a dog-eared thesaurus, and Malcolm's favorite floppy sailor hat. She lifted the cap to her nose. His fading scent invoked impressions of fatherly arms, a guiding hand, and loss. Anna tossed the hat on her couch and pressed fingers against teary eyes. Summoning strength, she pulled another item from the box. Malcolm's scrapbook of newspaper columns deserved a place of honor on her coffee table.

The rest of the items in the box were insignificant: a quilt from Anna's bed and a pillowcase stuffed with dirty clothes, leftovers from her trip. As Anna emptied the laundry from the box she spotted the cassette from Malcolm's answering machine lying on the bottom.

She recalled Investigator Corpizio asking her to listen to it again. *"Maybe something will come to you."*

Anna added it to her mental list of things to do.

Interrupted by a knock, she shoved the clutter aside and answered the door.

Addison Lee held his arms wide. "Anna, dear, I heard you were back." He stepped across the threshold and pulled her close to his bony shoulder. "I'm terribly sorry about your father. What an incredible loss."

Anna extracted herself from his embrace. "Nice to see you, Addison."

He peered intently at her. "How are you, dear? I mean, really?"

How should I be? "Fine," she said.

"Did you know that Randolph Harrington is in town? The man heard you speak at the Geneva Earth Summit. He's very impressed with you. Matter of fact, he wants you to be one of the speakers at the upcoming wilderness dedication."

Anna tried to muster an appreciative smile. "Would you like some tea or coffee?"

Backlit by the open door, Addison's white hair glowed. "Maybe later. I have good tidings! Our wolves have arrived for their orientation."

Anna brightened. "Where are they?"

"They've been placed in acclimation pens not far from the north entrance to Yellowstone."

"I want to see them."

"Naturally! I assumed you would be delighted." Addison beamed. "Work is just the medicine you need."

Anna grabbed a jacket and followed her mentor outside. "New car?" she asked climbing into the passenger seat of a tan Nissan Xterra SUV.

"He shot her a wry smile as he took his place behind the wheel. "I know what you're thinking."

"You do?"

"Of course darling Anna, you are so transparent. You are wondering why I am driving a vehicle, which wastes our natural resources?" Addison paused until he had safely backed down the driveway and steered onto to county road. "You see, I have reconciled myself to the demands of my vocation. Simply put—the nature of my calling demands a certain amount of compromise."

Anna bit her lip. "You don't need to explain yourself to me," she said, hoping her tone was not defensive. "I'm the last person who would pass judgment on you."

"You are simply going to fall in love with our wolves!" Addison trilled, "Nine males, and eight females, ranging from black to gorgeous silver. One, I've nick-named Anna—definitely an alpha." He said with a wink. "Oh yes, and there's an adorable pup, too."

"I can't wait to meet them."

"There's one little stop I need to make first," Addison said as he accelerated down the road. "I'm afraid you may find it a bit emotional."

"Why?"

"A local rancher passed away," he explained, "and I need to pay my respects."

"Who is it?"

"Duke Bassett, from the Broken Arrow Ranch." Addison gave Anna a sideways glance. "Did you know him?"

"Only by name. His ranch is in a beautiful spot."

"I couldn't agree with you more. Given the circumstances, I felt it would be prudent to offer the services and friendship of the Pristine Valley Nature Coalition."

Anna grew pensive as they parked beside the main lodge of the ranch, though she didn't know why.

Addison patted Anna's hand in a fatherly gesture. "I think it would be best if you wait in the car."

His condescending tone angered Anna. She

squared her shoulders and stepped from the vehicle with stubborn resolve. "I'm fine."

Addison's eyebrows shot up. "Whatever you think best."

Anna suppressed her irritation and followed him up the steps and through the door to the lobby.

Shouting issued from the back room. "You don't own me!" The voice sounded like that of a young male. A second later, a door slammed.

Anna leaned over to Addison and whispered, "This might not be a good time."

"On the contrary—it's a perfect time." He rang the front desk bell.

A petite middle-aged woman appeared, looking haggard. "Can I help you?"

Addison quickly made the introductions, and launched into condolences. "Mrs. Fischer, I'm here to offer my sincere sympathy over the death of your father."

The woman blinked, but showed no emotion. As if on cue, her face took on a pathetic pallor. "Call me Cassandra. Yes, it has been very difficult—almost more than I can take."

"I'm sure it is." He pulled Anna closer. "My young friend here has recently suffered the loss of her father. She understands exactly what you are going through."

Cassandra's eyes flicked to Anna and she fingered the ends of her smooth brown hair. Hard scowl lines appeared on the woman's pretty face. "I'm sorry to hear that."

Anna shot an irritated look toward Addison.

"If there is anything we can do," he said softly, "anything at all . . ."

A faint smile quivered over the woman's thin lips. "I appreciate your concern." Outside, a motor fired up. Through the window, Anna caught sight of a four-wheeler speeding across the lot, kicking up dust and sod. Cassandra hurried to the door, visibly tense.

Without missing a beat, Addison continued. "In times like this, friends can be invaluable."

"I'm sorry," Cassandra cut in with a dismissive tone, "but I'm really not up to visitors."

"That must have been your son," Addison said. "Teenagers can be such a challenge."

Cassandra's head bobbed in agreement. "You probably heard us having a little disagreement. Over my objections, Cordell has decided to take a summer job. Logging," she added with disdain.

Addison brightened. "Maybe I can help."

Cassandra studied him skeptically. "I don't see how."

"We represent an environmental group. Our interests may be more closely aligned than you realize."

Anna shifted nervously. She did not like where this was going.

"You are justifiably concerned about your son's choice of summer jobs. We are interested in putting an end to the logging business." Addison reached for Cassandra's hand and gave it a fatherly squeeze. "We can all work together, don't you think?"

The vulnerable woman considered Addison's bait with interest.

Addison set the hook. "Besides the political clout our organization enjoys, there are many fringe benefits that may help you at a time like this. We have a stable of experts who can bring clarity to estate issues. Inheritance tax and whatnot can be so confusing."

"I'd like to hear more," Cassandra said.

"There are many options, really. A conservation easement is one." He snapped his wrist over and checked his watch. "But now is not the time. I really must be going." Addison strolled towards the door but hesitated. "I just had an idea," he said smoothly. "The Pristine Valley Nature Coalition is having a meeting this Friday. I would love to escort you as my guest. Can I pick you up around seven?"

"I'd like that."

On the way to Yellowstone, Addison prattled on about fundraising and the upcoming wilderness dedication, and the wolves. "Things will soon be different," he said, "Our four-footed friends are the perfect catalyst for change."

"You mean they will help to balance the eco-system?"

"Much more than that, my dear!" Addison rolled to a stop at the entrance to Yellowstone National Park, flashed a Golden Age Passport to the ranger and was waived on through. "The wolves will help to usher in a new era of environmental control."

Pawns, Anna thought as Addison put his foot to the gas pedal and picked up speed. She stared from the window, her eyes unfocused on a blur of lodge pole pines that whizzed past. *So this is what the wolves have become . . .*

About ten miles inside the park, Addison steered his Xterra down a restricted-use-service road to a series of chain link holding pens. Anna hopped eagerly from the vehicle. Time spent with the canines would be a welcome respite. *At least the wolves don't pretend to be anything other than predators.*

CHAPTER 22

I'll not willingly offend, Nor be easily offended;
What's amiss I'll strive to mend,
And endure what can't be mended.
Issac Watts

Wyoming
Thursday, June 29

Grace made the morning rounds with coffeepot in hand. Business at the café had slacked off since the construction workers at the mansion had dwindled down to a skeleton crew of finish carpenters. Soon, life would return to normal. Grace welcomed the respite from kitchen duties. It gave her a chance to chat with the patrons.

On the far end of the counter, Pastor Charlie Waits sopped up his last bite of biscuits and gravy.

Grace poured him a fresh cup of coffee. "What brings you out so early this morning?"

Charlie wrapped his hands around the warm mug of coffee. "The hospital wants me to visit with one of their patients."

"Nothing serious, I hope." Grace said, clearing the pastor's dirty dish.

Milo breezed into the room.

"Morning, Milo," Charlie said. He cocked his head toward Grace. "The boy has a broken leg and some bruises, I think. He's lucky though. It could have been a lot worse."

"You talking about that idiot kid who fell off the cliff?" Milo interjected. "He had no business being up there in the first place."

Grace looked sharply at her husband. "The newspaper article said the young man was on a Native American Vision Quest," she said.

Charlie took a sip of coffee. "The boy is ready to be released, but he needs a place to stay until he's up to traveling. He's a member of the Crow nation, like I am."

"So they thought he'd be more comfortable among his own kind, huh? If you ask me, Pastor, you got rocks for brains."

Grace felt her face flush with embarrassment. "Nobody asked you, Milo!"

"Don't you have something to do in the kitchen?" he fired back.

Charlie stood and tossed a generous tip on the counter. "I think I'll go now and leave you two lovebirds to work things out." His warm brown eyes danced with humor. "We're having church out in the pasture this Sunday, under the shade of that old cottonwood. I'd love to see you both there."

Grace followed the pastor to the door. "That patient you're seeing. Is he the same young man who was in church last Sunday?"

"That's the one," he said. With a cheerful wave, he slipped through the door.

Grace fought the urge to run after Charlie, to warn him that this young man had been standing outside the café when it nearly burned down. *It's just a coincidence*, Grace told herself, but she couldn't shake the anxious feeling in the pit of her stomach.

—⚬⚬—

Thursday, June 29

On the steps of Charlie Waits' modest mobile home, Peter refused the pastor's offer to help. "I can do it myself." Peter tucked his crutches beneath his left arm and grasped the banister with his right hand. It wobbled precariously beneath his weight. He shifted his balance and a lightning bolt of pain shot up his bad leg. Peter sucked in a sharp breath.

"Gotta get that thing fixed," Charlie said with an apologetic tone. He hurried ahead and held the door open. "I'll fix meatloaf for dinner tonight. It's a specialty of mine."

Inside, Peter brushed long black strands of hair from his face and glanced around the cluttered living room. It was the last place he wanted to be. "If I had a choice, I'd be long gone by now," he grumbled.

The pastor looked at him. "It's been rough. I bet you're tired." Charlie pointed down the hallway. "Your bedroom is the first door to the right. I tried to make it comfortable. You've got your own bathroom, so that should make things easier for you."

Peter hobbled to the room and closed the door.

"Let me know if there's anything I can get you," the pastor called from the hallway.

Peter listened as the man shuffled away. He lowered his body to the bed and placed a pillow under his throbbing leg. He slipped a black-and-white snapshot from his pocket and held it in a patch of window light. He had studied the image a thousand times. On dark days, it had sparked hope, a sense of belonging.

"The dream is dead," Peter whispered bitterly. His fingers curled around the brittle paper and he hurled it to the floor.

CHAPTER 23

Seasons may roll, but the true soul
Burns the same where'er it goes.
Thomas Moore

Wyoming
Friday, June 30

    With one eye on the rearview mirror, Dillon shifted to low and angled slowly around the treacherous switchbacks, being careful not to rock his trailer from its hitch. The Kragler Pass road had always been a bad one, made even worse by last year's rains. Flash flooding that year had all but wiped out patches of the narrow, rocky road.

    Dillon grumbled as his tires crept over jagged rocks. Kragler Pass was never more than a fallback spot for his timbering business. He still couldn't believe things had come to this. But with a log quota hanging over his head and bills to pay, Dillon pushed on over deep ruts and fallen debris.

The trip to the top of the mountain was tedious and slow. Dillon wiped his brow and breathed a sigh of relief as the truck rounded the last knob. He steered down a small ravine toward a dense stand of trees, trying to remember the last time he had been there. Years ago. Dillon looked over the terrain. Miles of dead pine with dry red needles littered the mountain, indicating a pine beetle infestation. The whole area was a veritable tinderbox of fire fuel.

He climbed from the truck, removed his baseball cap, and scratched his head. How, he wondered, could he eek a quota of lumber from this diseased forest? Thinning cuts produced healthier forest, better able to resist the parasitic bugs. Now, most of the dead standing trees were only good for firewood.

He laughed at the irony. This area was off limits to firewood-cutting permits. Maybe there was logic in the management policies, but they made no sense to him.

Dillon replaced his cap and surveyed his options. Near the edge of a clearing, he spotted a target tree, retrieved the chainsaw from the back of the truck, and was just about to fire it up when the sound of a whirring motor turned his head.

"Everybody knows this is my timber sale," he muttered.

Anger propelled Dillon to the edge of the clearing to have a look—maybe catch a bootleg logging outfit in the act. He caught sight of a four-wheeler bouncing over the far side of the meadow and shaded his eyes from the sun to get a better look. "Well, I'll be darned."

"Uncle Dillon," Cordell called over the hum of the engine. The teenager closed the gap between them in less than a minute and slid to a stop beside the old pickup. "I'm here to work."

"I thought you couldn't make it. I figured with your Grandpa Duke passing away . . ."

Cordell peeled off his helmet and tossed it to the ground next to his four-wheeler. "Mom called, didn't she?"

Dillon nodded. "Yeah. She's not too happy about you working for me."

"Is that all?" The teenager slipped a backpack from his shoulder and rummaged through it. He produced a mason jar filled with gray powder. "I thought maybe she realized that I took some of Grandpa's ashes."

"You what?"

"Mom had him cremated," Cordell explained.

Dillon pulled a blade of grass from a clump at his feet and stuck it between his teeth. "Don't you think you should wait for a family service or something?"

"Mom told me there's not going to be a funeral." The boy shrugged. "Grandpa once said, when it was his time to go, he wanted his ashes spread in the mountains." Cordell looked around reflectively. "I figured this is as good a place as any."

Dillon smiled. The boy was a lot like his dad. Reuben could be as stubborn as a knot-headed mule.

—⁓—

Wyoming
Friday, June 30

There was a grizzly nearby. Reuben could tell. The animal's pungent musk hung like moss in a bog. He took a step, scanning the dark mountain tarn for movement. There wasn't much time. Reuben was sure his trackers were not far behind. He imagined them closing in with the same stealth that he employed.

A dog bayed over the rise and Reuben's breathing quickened. *Take cover,* he told himself.

Up ahead, an old tree had fallen across a shallow pond, its bows rising from the water like the Loch Ness monster. Reuben slogged across the murky pool and crouched near the trunk. In the shallow water, he knelt behind a branch and peered out from between its dead pine needles. Ripples from his movement went out like radar. He willed them to stop, drew in controlled breaths, and waited.

The water returned to mossy glass. Mosquitoes danced about Reuben's head and something slimy brushed past his knee.

On the other side of the thicket, a branch broke and a hound dog bayed. The animal bounded into view. Reuben forced himself to remain calm as the animal sniffed and scratched about the bramble. Just over the rise, he heard more barking. Two, maybe three hounds, he figured. If they caught Reuben's scent, it would all be over.

Just beyond the tangle of brush, a commotion erupted. Reuben heard water splashing, growls, and an eerie, high-pitched cry that sounded almost human. *Bear cub, probably.*

A moment later a man's voice shouted orders. "Off. Off!"

The other hounds arrived. Reuben closed his eyes, visualizing the pandemonium that was in progress just out of sight.

Suddenly a grizzly cub burst through the thicket and did a belly flop in the shallow pond. The dogs ran near the shore, barking manically while the quivering cub sent out a pathetic, almost chilling cry.

A stocky man appeared, snapping orders at the dogs. They whimpered in protest and reluctantly obeyed. Warily, Reuben watched the tracker raise his field glasses and sweep the mountain tarn with an expert eye. He tensed as the field glasses turned his way.

Behind the tracker, Reuben saw an explosion of movement. The man turned and found himself face to face with an angry sow grizzly.

The man went for his holstered pistol, but it was too late. The bear was on him in an instant, roaring, her snout drawn back in maternal indignation. With one powerful swing, the sow sent the man flying through the air. She turned on the dogs. They barked furiously, alternately lunging at the angry animal and pulling back in fear. Drool dripped from the grizzly's teeth and she rumbled with rage.

"Shoot! Shoot it!" the man screamed as his friends arrived on the scene. One leveled a twelve gauge, caught the bear in his sights, and fired. *Hoowooomp.* Reuben recognized the distinctive sound of a rubber bullet.

The grizzly yelped in pain, and bolted through the trees with the cub on her heals. The dogs, lathered and yelping, took chase.

The men were well equipped with mountain gear and layered clothing. They reminded Reuben of an elite military unit, but there were no identifying marks on their shirts or jackets.

"It's a pretty deep cut, but you'll be okay," one of the men assured his injured friend. He turned to the others. "We need to get him back to town."

The sound of barking faded in the distance as the trackers carried the injured man from the bog.

Reuben let out a relieved sigh. In the commotion, his pursuers had forgotten him, at least for now.

CHAPTER 24

Something hidden. Go and find it.
Go, and look behind the Ranges—
Something lost behind the Ranges.
Lost and waiting for you. . . Go!
—Rudyard Kipling

Wyoming

Saturday, July 1

Anna dumped the pile of mail on the kitchen table, determined to conquer her procrastination. She rolled up her sleeves and swept the junk mail into a trash can. Anna set aside the bills and focused on the cards, separating condolences from those congratulating her for the honors bestowed upon her at the Earth Summit. It seemed unfair that the proudest moment in Anna's life was followed by the saddest.

She turned one card over in her hand, trying to decide in which category it belonged. It contained a personal note from Gabor Gagne. "I share your loss," he wrote. "Please take all the time you need to reconsider my job offer. The Endangered Earth Alliance would greatly benefit from your special insight and zeal."

It was a tempting offer. Yet Anna's current work was unfinished. Years of planning had gone into the wolf reintroduction, and the dream was now close to realization. She shook her head, tossed the letter into the trash can and worked through the rest of the pile with haste.

The last piece of mail was a large manila envelope. She lifted it, considering its Maine postmark. With a feeling of unease, she lifted the clasp.

The phone rang and Anna froze—three rings and then a hang-up, just like before. The calls had been coming with regularity, all registering Public Phone on the caller ID.

Anna tossed the envelope aside and turned on the burner under the tea kettle. She would fix a cup of chamomile to calm her nerves and then call the phone company to report the harassing calls.

The phone rang again. This time, six rings, before the answering machine switched on. After a few seconds of raspy breathing, the caller spoke. "Did you get the envelope?"

Anna lunged for the receiver, but the man hung up.

It was Vonsetter. She was sure of it. Anna felt her throat tighten and a sickening feeling crawled over her flesh. She stared at the envelope on the table, suddenly afraid to open it. It could be a bomb or maybe even anthrax.

Anna carefully ran her fingers over the paper, trying to detect anything unusual. She mustered her courage and pried opened the clasp. Peeking inside, she saw a large hardbound book. She reached in and pulled out a Dartmouth yearbook. The binding was cracked and frayed and some of the pages torn. Anna thought of her own college yearbook, stored in the bottom of a box somewhere, seldom opened. Vonsetter had apparently spent some time reminiscing.

Anna fanned the pages, looking for a note hidden within, anything to explain why Vonsetter had sent her this mysterious package. She found nothing.

She turned the book over and looked at the cover. It was from the year Malcolm graduated from Dartmouth. After a few seconds of page flipping, she found her father's photo among the graduating class. On a hunch, she turned a few more pages until she reached the Vs.

William Vonsetter! Smooth faced and youthful, but with those same wild eyes.

The tea kettle shrieked and Anna jumped. With her heart pounding, she found Corpizio's number and dialed.

—∧∧—

Maine
Monday, July 3

Investigator Corpizio sat at the office desk with fingertips pressed together, his mind turning angles. He had been that way for more than an hour, frustrated that he had been unable to give Anna O'Neil encouraging news about the investigation into her father's murder. Questions, like puzzle pieces, shifted around his thoughts, yet none fit. Why was Malcolm killed and what prompted the killer to return to Canaan Island on the night Detective Dobbs was killed? It all came down to motives. Corpizio drew a blank.

Someone knocked lightly and Corpizio looked up.

"Excuse me, sir." A rookie officer with a crew cut offered the investigator a piece of paper. "Here's the list of Dartmouth alumni from the year you requested. The ones I marked are deceased; a few haven't been located yet."

"Make the calls and narrow the list. When you're done, give it back to me," Corpizio said. "What about Anna O'Neil's telephone record?"

"The phone company is still analyzing that information, but the profile on William Vonsetter is in."

The investigator leaned forward, half bored. He did not need a profile to convince him the man was unbalanced. "Thanks. Just set it on the desk."

The officer hesitated.

"Anything else?" Corpizio asked.

"Sir, some of the people around the office are passing the hat for Detective Dobbs's family—you know, to help with funeral expenses."

Morale in the office had been low since their comrade's death—Corpizio could feel the heaviness. "Count me in," he said, watching the rookie amble away.

He lifted a stack of newspaper clippings: Malcolm O'Neil's most recent columns. Maybe, if he could find the subject of O'Neil's last column, a motive would surface. It wasn't going to be easy, for the victim's desk had been rummaged. O'Neil's notes were missing and the computer drive wiped clean. Obviously someone did not want that information found.

Corpizio tossed the article back on the desk and thumbed through the stack until he found Malcolm O'Neil's phone-company log. It yielded several clues to the possible subject matter.

The investigator had already checked out several of the leads. The call to the Environmental Protection Agency proved to be a dead end. "The black hole of bureaucracy," he said aloud.

Corpizio felt his shirt pocket for his notebook, retrieved it, and flipped it open to refresh his memory. The Maine Fish and Game Department had been more cooperative. O'Neil had called to inquire about a recent wolf sighting in the northern part of the state. Corpizio turned another page.

Gabor Gagne of the Endangered Earth Alliance

could not be reached, but an associate remembered the call. Mr. O'Neil was writing a profile on the organization's successes.

Corpizio closed his notebook.

His memory of the last entry needed no prompting. It was a call to a detective agency. Malcolm O'Neil had initiated contact with William Vonsetter—an action that may have cost the columnist his life.

Yet, the investigator couldn't shake the feeling that something was amiss. Vonsetter was like a puzzle piece so close in shape and color that it appeared to fit, and yet . . .

He summoned the office secretary. "See if you can get a hold of Gerri Redding at state headquarters. Tell her she can't retire just yet; I need her help."

CHAPTER 25

A quiet life, which was not life at all.
Elizabeth Barrett Browning

Wyoming

Tuesday, July 4th

The mansion's indoor swimming pool had become one of Lily's favorite places. In the water's soft embrace, she floated on her back, watching beads of moisture clinging to the rafters like diamonds. It was quiet there—maybe too quiet. Lily's restless thoughts were catching up with her.

She climbed from the pool and wrapped a Turkish towel around her body, wondering how to pass the next few hours. It was the Fourth of July, but Lily didn't feel like driving to Cedar Ridge to watch a small town parade.

She sighed and looked to her left at the basement's corridor. Randolph was having treatments for leukemia in the room he had insisted "must never be mentioned."

Lily turned to her right and made her way to the glass doors, opened them and stepped onto an outdoor deck, which butted up against the base of the mountain. She padded on bare feet across the tiered redwood deck. Lily chose a spot built around a tumbling stream and sank into a lounge chair, allowing the afternoon sunshine to warm her. Birds chattered in the trees. A pinecone dropped nearby. Life was all around, yet Lily felt detached. She looked blankly at the beautiful house that she shared with Randolph. It didn't feel like home—nothing did. Lily tossed the towel from her shoulders, wishing she knew what "home" felt like. Growing up as a foster child had taught her the rules of survival; only perfect little girls are loved, so don't make waves. Sometimes she wondered if her husband really loved her. *How could he?* Lily felt sick to her stomach. She closed her eyes and steadied her breathing.

"There you are, Wildflower." Randolph joined her on the deck, draped his gaze across her lithe figure, and licked his lips. "I thought I'd find you here." He sat at her feet and laid a hand on her leg. "Paradise, don't you think?" He drew in a deep cleansing breath. "I am one with nature here, stronger." Randolph stood. "Oh, by the way, I hired a western clothing designer to tailor a new wardrobe for you. I've already approved the styles, so all you need to do is give the designer your measurements." Randolph looked pleased with himself. "You will have a new image to present."

Lily forced the expected smile and fought another wave of nausea.

—⟋⟍—

Wyoming
Tuesday, July 4

Peter leaned over his bowl of rice cereal, feeling like a prisoner. Between bites, he studied Charlie, quickly dropping his gaze when the old man looked his way.

"Did you sleep well?"

Peter responded with a grunt.

"Happy Fourth of July," the pastor said as he drew back the drapes and looked outside. The view from the mobile home window showcased the burnt-out remains of the barn, but that didn't seem to diminish Charlie's enthusiasm. "There's a parade in town today. Want to go?"

Peter dropped his spoon. It disappeared into the bowl. He considered fishing for it, but instead pushed the cereal bowl aside.

"If you want a ride, I'm going into town this morning anyway. The city administrators have agreed to let me borrow some folding chairs from the auditorium for church next Sunday." The pastor's eyebrows shot up and his face brightened. "We're having a worship service Friday afternoon, down by the river. You're welcome to come."

Peter glared at the old man.

"Why are you so angry?" Charlie asked.

The seconds boiled with tension. Finally, Peter spoke. "What do you think is the first thing people see when they look at me?"

Charlie smiled. "A handsome young man."

"You know what they see—a Native American. If they're being politically correct, that is."

"You should be proud of your heritage," Charlie said. "Being a Native American is nothing to be ashamed of."

"Look who's talking!" Peter tossed his head contemptuously. "Don't you dare talk to me about heritage."

Charlie offered a patient look, which made Peter loathe him even more.

"You offend me with your so-called righteousness!"

The pastor drew in a sharp breath. "I don't think of myself as righteous." He shook his head. "I'm just a man who needs God." He bent over to tie his shoelace.

"Yeah—the white man's God! How could you turn your back on the Native American people?" Peter felt invigorated by the challenge.

Charlie appeared thoughtful. "I love my people and their rich history. But I found another heritage—one that's not of this world. This 'white man's God' cares about men's hearts."

Peter laughed. "Right! He just likes Anglo hearts better."

"You're wrong," Charlie said gently. "If you took the time to understand God, you would know." The pastor looked down at his hands. "There was a time when my life was a wreck. I hurt everyone I loved. But now, because of God's grace, I can wake up every morning and know that I'm forgiven."

"Yeah, and what makes you so special?" Peter asked, folding his arms across his chest.

"Absolutely nothing," Charlie answered. "When I came to Jesus, I had reached the bottom. My wife had left me. My health was shot. I was an alcoholic. I had no pride left to prop me up. Even my own people couldn't help me. So I prayed." He pondered for a moment. "You know, I didn't really expect God to show up for someone like me, but he did. And I've been grateful ever since."

"Where's your wife now?" Peter caught a fleeting glimpse of pain in the pastor's eyes.

"I don't really know," Charlie said. "She left years ago."

"Kids?"

"No." Charlie lowered himself to the table. "I've told you all about me. What about you, Peter?"

"My mother was a drunk, just like you. She died in an alley behind her favorite bar."

"And your father?"

Hatred welled in Peter's bosom, so deep and intense that it frightened him. "Let's just say he never wanted me, okay?"

"You must forgive," Charlie said.

Peter propped his crutches under his arms and hoisted himself up. "Never," he said as he hobbled away.

—ɰ—

Wyoming

Tuesday evening, July 4th

Dillon stuck his Chevy truck in low gear, applied the brakes, and listened to them squeal in protest. The Kragler Pass road was steep. In his rearview mirror, he watched his loaded trailer cantering precariously over the ruts. He carefully turned the wheel around a sharp corner of the switchback, trying not to let momentum take control.

Without warning, the truck lurched violently to the left side. Dillon jammed his foot on the brakes. It felt soft and unresponsive. The trailer pushed the truck forward like a locomotive. Dillon cranked the steering wheel hard to the right. The trailer jackknifed. The half-ton truck bounced sideways like a toy.

Dillon glanced back as the trailer swung toward the edge of the road. White fear swept over him. Without thinking, he jerked the emergency brake. He cut the engine and bailed from the truck to the gravel road. He landed hard against the packed ground. Dillon watched the scene unfold. Almost in slow motion, the trailer shaved away the embankment. Just short of going over, it ground to a stop.

Dillon scrambled to his feet and hurried to the edge to inspect the trailer. Half of its belly teetered over blue sky. It rocked and groaned. Dirt crumbled from the unstable bank.

Dillon knelt on shaky knees for a better look. His truck was high-centered on a scrap of roadside rock. That was all that kept the whole rig from plummeting down a fifty-foot drop.

Dillon's throat tightened as he considered his options. If the trailer went over, the truck would go with it. If he unhooked the trailer, there was a risk of disturbing the balance. He opted to leave it alone.

He stepped back, let a string of unsavory words escape from his lips, and fought the urge to kick a tire. It was flat anyway. Dillon checked the others and discovered three more flats—one on the trailer.

A subtle hissing sound met his ear. He followed the source and discovered two nails embedded deep within the rubber.

Somebody had put nails on the road! With a surge of adrenaline, Dillon curled his fist into a ball. "This is gonna stop!" he screamed into the mountain air. His words echoed back.

With an angry stride, Dillon marched down the road. A half mile into his trek, a searing pain shot up his leg. Dillon dropped to the ground. An inspection of his work boot revealed a nail driven through his heel. He pulled out his pocketknife and pried the imbedded nail from the sole. Dillon shed his boot to examine the wound. His foot throbbed. The puncture felt deep, yet it wasn't bleeding, making infection a possibility.

Dillon slipped his boot back on, re-laced it, and began a slow and painful descent from the mountain.

The sun was sinking in the sky. It would take hours to reach the main road and another five miles to the Fischer Creek Café. He limped on, vacillating between anger and gratitude. Down below, the pop of fireworks erupted—reminding Dillon that it was the 4th of July. Bottle rockets whistled across the dusky sky and an occasional burst of color exploded in the valley raining down sparkling streamers. The display seemed strange— *surreal*, Dillon thought, almost like a celebration for his life, which had nearly ended on the mountain.

CHAPTER 26

A few honest men are better than numbers.
Oliver Cromwell

Maine
Wednesday, July 5

Investigator Corpizio paced around the long table where he had gathered evidence. The collection of information had swelled to the point of being intimidating and weariness was beginning to set in.

"Building a scrapbook, Jay?"

He turned as a matronly looking woman breezed into the room. He threw his arms wide to welcome his old partner. "Gerri, what a surprise!"

"Don't give me that, you sly fox," she scolded. "You knew I'd come back in a pinch. But don't think this means I'm giving up on my retirement." She peeled off a fuzzy sweater and tossed it on a chair. "This is just a little detour, that's all." Gerri lowered her voice. "Between you and me, it couldn't have come at a better time. My husband has decided he's a world-class fisherman and he says nobody can gut and clean trout like me."

"Sounds fishy," Corpizio said with a grin.

His old partner rolled her eyes and sashayed across the room. Gerri pulled up her sleeves and poured herself a cup of black coffee. "I'm ready to burn the midnight oil."

Jay looked fondly at the doughy grandmother. As far as he was concerned, Gerri Redding had been one of the Maine bureau's best-kept secret weapons.

She took a sip and inspected the clippings on the table. "So, what do you have?"

"This paper trail represents a man named William Vonsetter." Corpizio motioned to a cluttered display to his right.

"Tell me about him."

"He's a genius, a physicist by profession. You know the type: a mind that flies way over the heads of most of us."

Gerri nodded and blew on her coffee. "And sometimes just keeps going and going. Is he a loner?"

"Yeah, but he didn't start out that way. Vonsetter and the victim were friends in college and remained close for about ten years, until they had some kind of a falling out." He opened the Dartmouth yearbook and pointed to the photo of Malcolm and Vonsetter.

Gerri read the caption. "Ecology Club—before it was really vogue." She leaned closer and pointed to one of the figures in the photo. "Who's this hairy caveman?"

"Name's Jeffery Lyons." Corpizio stared at a spot on the wall, trying to recall something that was said.

"What are you thinking?" Gerri asked.

"I had a conversation with one of the victim's old college acquaintances. When I asked the guy about Vonsetter, Lyons, and O'Neil, he said the craziest one of the bunch was Jeffery Lyons."

"Might be worth exploring," Gerri said. "Even though the guy's probably a boring CPA with five kids."

Jay flipped to the class pictures and took a long look at Jeffery Lyons. "I haven't been able to locate this guy."

"Everybody can be found. We'll just keep looking. Now, tell me about our transient Einstein."

"William Vonsetter's life seemed to take a nosedive after he worked on a global warming summit." Corpizio selected a couple of clippings from the table and handed them to Gerri.

"Physicist Claims Misappropriation of Scientific Information," she read aloud. " 'It's a sham,' Vonsetter charges."

"I have Vonsetter pegged as a whistle-blower type," Corpizio said.

"So what came of the whole," Gerri held up the article and squinted her eyes, "Global Warming Summit?" She dropped the clippings back on the table.

"Nothing. Vonsetter's claims were dismissed as ramblings. After that, he just seemed to fade away."

"Until?" Gerri coaxed.

"Malcolm O'Neil managed to locate him with the help of a private investigator."

"Bad move for the victim." Gerri cringed. "So, why did he try to find him after all these years?"

"Wish I knew. The private investigator wasn't very helpful." Corpizio scratched his cheek. "We know he was in the area around the time of the murder."

"William Vonsetter sounds like he's on some kind of delusional mission." Gerri swilled down some coffee.

"That's what worries me," Corpizio said. "Especially since he's been in contact with the victim's daughter, Anna O'Neil."

Gerri's thin eyebrows rose. "You think she's in danger?"

Corpizio didn't answer, but a bad feeling lodged in the pit of his stomach.

"What are these?" the woman asked. She scooped up another stack of papers and thumbed through them.

"The victim's recent phone contacts. I'm trying to piece together the last column he was working on. The hard drive on his computer was erased."

"Interesting," Gerri said, studying the papers in hand. "The Maine Fish and Game Department, the Environmental Protection Agency, and the Endangered Earth Alliance."

"I spoke with all of them. Nothing there—just loose ends."

"You know what they say." She smiled. "If you pull on the right thread, things might unravel."

"I figure O'Neil was preparing to write an article that would humiliate Vonsetter." Corpizio felt Gerri staring at him. "I have a feeling O'Neil was working on something that Vonsetter took personally." The rest went without saying. To an unbalanced mind that could be a reason to kill.

"You still haven't learned to trust your instincts," Gerri said, dropping the papers back onto the table. "I know you, Jay. If you really thought there was nothing here, all this clutter wouldn't still be sitting on the table."

Corpizio stared at the evidence table. "You're right. Now all we have to do is find out who else had a motive."

—◊—

Wyoming
Wednesday, July 5

Alone in her cabin, Anna pressed her ear against the receiver and thought she could detect the faint sounds of shallow breathing. "Who is this?"

The breathing quickened. "Don't hang up."

It was his voice. "Vonsetter, what do you want with me?"

"Shouldn't have said my name." His words faded to a whisper. "Phone might not be secure. Did you get the package?"

"Yes, but I don't understand . . ."

"Keep it with you. Don't trust anyone." The pitch of his voice rose. "Can't say any more."

"Did you kill my father?" Anna blurted. She heard an audible gasp on the other end of the line.

"That what they told you?" Vonsetter evaded the question. "It started with the panel—never ends."

"Panel?" Anna asked cautiously

"Geneva Global Warming Summit. That's when I realized something was amiss. Tried to tell Malcolm . . ." His words dropped away.

Anna was afraid this strange man might slip through her fingers again. She had to keep him talking. "What happened at the summit?"

Vonsetter required no further coaxing. His story pulsed rapidly through the telephone receiver. "After the second session, conclusions were submitted. They selected scientists to draft the final report. The rest of us they dismissed. Second panel all supported extreme global warming theories—no objective counterpoints—no majority consensus." Vonsetter inhaled. "A sham! A ruse!"

"I've seen the data on global warming," Anna said with forced calm. "As a scientist, I see nothing that I question."

Unnerving, machine-gun-like laughter erupted through the receiver. "You never asked the right questions—the questions asked by the first panel."

"I don't know what you're talking about."

"Exactly my point," Vonsetter yelped. "First panel of scientists issued a report—it disappeared."

"Are you saying that global warming is a hoax?"

"Temperatures fluctuate. That's not in dispute. Question is—why?" Vonsetter's voice lowered to a throaty whisper. "One narrow view was advanced: Manmade greenhouse gases are responsible for these fluctuations. All other evidence was disregarded."

"So you don't believe that carbon dioxide emissions are contributing to rising atmospheric temperatures?"

"They're not entirely to blame. Ninety percent of global warming took place in a five-year period, from 1917 through 1921. Very few manmade emissions in those days. Most carbon dioxide emissions occurred after the 1950s. Explain that." He paused to await Anna's response. After a long silence, he continued. "By the early '70s, greenhouse gases were increasing. Global temperatures fell." Vonsetter burst into laughter. "Remember the headlines? Planet Plunging into Ice Age!"

The line grew quiet. Anna strained her ear.

"In the '80s, ground-level weather station data determined that earth's surface temperatures had appeared to increase."

"I remember reading about that."

"Bet you never saw anything about concurrent satellite data. They showed no changes in the temperature of the earth's atmosphere."

Anna's thoughts started spinning. The man's argument was compelling. But, Anna reminded herself, Vonsetter might be a murderer.

"Check for yourself," he said. "Tree-ring analysis doesn't lie. No noticeable temperature fluctuations for a quarter of a century. I could talk about ozone depletion too—but no time." Vonsetter cleared his throat. "Good news was kept hidden. Why?"

She massaged her temple. "If what you're saying is credible, there must be other scientists who agree."

"I'm not alone."

"Others can verify your story?" Anna twisted the telephone cord in her fingers.

"I need to go."

"Wait." Anna leaned forward in her chair. "What does this have to do with my father?"

"Malcolm was ready for truth. That's why he found me."

Anna sat up straight. "My father contacted you?"

"I knew things. I had information he needed."

"What?"

"Already said too much. Be careful. There's danger everywhere. Remember what I told you."

In the next moment, Anna sat staring at the receiver, listening to the dial tone. Was Vonsetter's warning of danger real? Or the delusional threats of a lunatic?

CHAPTER 27

For this my son was dead, and is alive again;
he was lost and is found.
Luke 15:24

Wyoming
Thursday, July 6

By the time the last of the breakfast crowd trickled out the door of the Fischer Creek Café, Grace felt exhausted. More from trying to keep up with her daughter-in-law's incessant chatter than from the tourists whose bus had just rolled out.

"Florida," Jody said, looking out the window. "That's what the license plate says. Must not be big tippers in Florida." She pulled out the empty pockets of her jeans. "Can you believe that whole group left me a measly ten dollars? They had me running my feet off too."

Grace smiled absently. "That's nice, honey."

"I'm positive that blue-haired lady ordered a traveler's special, not pancakes like she claimed." Jody rolled her eyes. "But the customer is always right."

"At her age, maybe she just forgot," Grace suggested and busied herself placing fresh-baked pies in the display cooler.

Jody sighed and plopped down at the counter. "I'm getting kind of worried about Dillon and Milo. They should be back by now. I hope they're not in trouble. That husband of mine lay awake in bed all last night thinking about how to get that truck and trailer safely off the pass. He said they'd probably have to brace things up and try to unload the trailer, but the hitch is broken. Just what we need right now! It'll probably take days to fix." Jody drew a breath and glared at her wristwatch. "Hope nothing went wrong."

"They're probably just being extra careful," Grace said. "You know how safety conscious your father-in-law is."

"Milo is a worry wart! No offense." Jody giggled, but her concerned gaze shifted back to the window. "Hello. Look who just pulled in."

A green Forest Service truck braked to a stop, and the sheriff pulled in beside it. Two men got out of the vehicles and had a short conversation in the parking lot.

Grace watched them approach the café.

"They've got a lot of nerve, coming here after the way they've given us the runaround," Jody snorted. "Word is, there are law-enforcement people crawling all over the mountains, tracking Reuben down like he's an animal."

She strung the words together rapidly as the men walked across the porch. "I heard one of the government guys got swiped by a grizzly." She smirked. "Serves him right!"

Grace wrinkled her brow at her daughter-in-law, but there was no time for a reprimand. The front door swung open and the two men walked in.

"Mornin', Grace," the sheriff said, respectfully removing his cowboy hat.

"Hello, Hodge," she said with a nod.

The men sat near the front door.

Jody clicked past them with a frosty air. The coffeepot was in her hand, but she offered none.

"Honey," Grace said, stepping forward and resting a hand on Jody's shoulder, "would you take over in the kitchen for a little while?"

The young woman relinquished the coffeepot, reluctantly grabbed an apron from a hook, and tied it around her skinny waist. She fired a dirty look over her shoulder before disappearing through the swinging door.

Grace offered the men menus and filled their mugs. "I heard you had a bit of trouble up on the mountain," she said. "I hope no one was hurt."

The ranger's eyebrow rose. "Word travels fast."

"It always has in the good town of Cedar Ridge," Sheriff Hodge said. He looked up at Grace. "You're right. Heard tell it got a bit 'western' up there. Could've been a whole lot worse."

Grace looked intently at the forest ranger. "Have you seen my son?"

The abruptness of the question seemed to startle him and he fumbled for words. "I'm sorry, ma'am, but that's classified information."

"For cryin' out loud," the sheriff cut in. "The Fischers are good people. I've known the family for years, and I ain't gonna ride my high horse on this case until I hear Reuben's side of the story." The sheriff looked softly at the worried mother. "He's alive, Grace. I can tell you that much. They've found up some signs."

"Thank God." Tears welled in Grace's eyes.

The forest ranger shot a disapproving look at the sheriff. He turned back to Grace. "We're doing everything we can to find your son, but so far, he's been very proficient at evading our attempts. That's what I wanted to talk to you about."

Grace folded her arms across her chest.

"We have no way of knowing what Reuben's next move will be, but if he should show up here . . ."

"Just what are your intentions, young man?" Grace cut in. "Do you think my son is a murderer?"

There was an awkward moment of silence before the man spoke. "We believe that Reuben knows what happened to Duke Bassett. We don't understand why your son is trying to avoid us, but we just want to clear things up. In order to do that, we need to speak to him."

"My son is innocent," Grace said emphatically. "And if Reuben shows up here, I'm sure he'll tell you that himself."

The screen door banged open and Milo stepped inside, his face animated with rage. Behind him, Dillon limped into the café.

"Look what the coyotes dragged in," Milo bellowed. He pointed his finger at the two lawmen. "You got a lot of nerve, ploppin' your fannies down at one of our tables."

Grace felt her face flush with embarrassment as the men stood to leave.

Sheriff Hodge slipped on his hat and nodded toward her.

"If you want to make yourselves useful," Milo growled, "I suggest you take a little ride up to Kragler Pass and find out who's been laying nails out on the road." He swept his arm toward his youngest son. "Dillon here 'bout got killed yesterday morning. What are you gonna do about that?"

"We'll check it out."

The sheriff cast a look of pity in Grace's direction as he made his exit.

She returned a grateful nod. The visit had brought her a measure of peace—at least Reuben was alive.

CHAPTER 28

Earth's crammed with heaven,
And every common bush afire with God;
The rest sit round it and pluck blackberries,
And daub their natural faces unaware . . .
Elizabeth Barrett Browning

Wyoming
Friday, July 7

Lily Harrington stood at the far end of the mansion's grand room, watching her husband barking orders at his staff. Nothing had changed since the last time she passed through except the shadows cast by the cathedral windows. Randolph still sat like a pale squire, holding court among his administrative assistants—"dutiful subjects," as Randolph often referred to them. All morning, he had been on the phone, calling in favors from across the country.

"The wilderness dedication will be a media extravaganza," Lily heard him say. "I envision celebrities and high-level politicians. . . I don't care how, just do it!" Randolph slammed down the receiver.

Seizing the opportunity, Lily stepped forward. Her husband looked up and held out his hand as if it were a scepter. His critical eye swept over Lily and he frowned. "You're not wearing one of your new western outfits."

Lily caught a glimpse of her reflection in an ornamental mirror: boots, khakis, and a simple blouse. "I was hoping to go into Cedar Ridge and check out some of the shops."

Randolph's frown remained in place.

"The new wardrobe is very nice, really." Lily licked her lips and forced a smile. "I just want to blend in."

Randolph seemed to ponder his wife's words. In the glow of the window, beads of sweat glistened on his lip. He looked tired. "Wildflower, if you were the type who just blends in, you never would have caught my eye. You are my wife after all and that makes you extraordinary."

The phone rang. Harrington's special assistant answered.

"I can't possibly go to town right now," Randolph said. "You'll have to go without me. I'll call the chauffeur."

"I'd like to drive myself," she said quickly. "If you don't mind."

"Oh, yes, of course—you want to blend in." Randolph tossed her the keys and took the telephone receiver from his assistant. "You've lined up a Hollywood face and a senator? Wonderful."

Lily slipped outside, feeling like a teenager with her daddy's car keys as she climbed behind the wheel of the Cadillac Escalade. She rolled down the windows as she drove. There was so much to explore. Wyoming was like an untamed wilderness. At the foot of the mountain, she turned onto the main road and gunned the engine, letting the smell of pine and sagebrush blow through her hair.

Just over a hill, the light on the dashboard blinked, catching her attention. *Empty!* Panic gripped Lily's stomach. She hadn't thought to check the gas gauge and it was probably fifteen miles to Cedar Ridge. Around the bend, the Fischer Creek Café and Gas Station came into view. Lily breathed a sigh of relief.

She gassed up and continued on her way, but a few miles later, the SUV shuddered and coughed. It died just as she pulled along the road's shoulder. Lily turned the key. The engine started with a rumble and died again.

Lily's fingers trembled as she fumbled for her cell phone. Randolph would be disappointed in her. He hated weakness of any kind. She dialed, but in the shadow of the mountains, there was no signal.

"Got car trouble?" A round-faced man pulled his truck alongside the SUV.

"I don't know what's wrong," Lily said, noticing the man's long braid. "It's brand new."

The Good Samaritan parked his truck and strolled around the Cadillac. "This is an odd day," he said, scratching his head. "There's another vehicle broke down a few miles from here." He held out his hand. "My name is Charlie Waits. I pastor a little fellowship that meets up the road, the Church of the Rock." He gave Lily an apologetic look. "I'm afraid I don't know much about cars."

The years had taught Lily that most people could not be trusted, yet this man's soft demeanor put her at ease. "I read something in the local paper about a church burning down. Was that yours?"

"Just the building burned," Charlie said with a smile. "The people still come and I figure they're the real church." He pointed to the back of his truck, loaded with folding chairs. I'm on my way there now."

"But it's not Sunday. Besides where will you meet?"

"Friday is just as good a day to worship as Sunday. We're all meeting down by the river," Charlie said. "There's a stand of cottonwoods, plenty of shade, and enough fresh air to go around. Who knows, we might even have a baptism or two."

Lily liked the man's optimism.

"If you want to join us, I'd be glad to give you a ride to your house afterwards. I'd take you home now, but I'm running late."

She looked down the lonely stretch of road and considered her limited options.

"The more the merrier." Charlie grinned.

Lily agreed and climbed into his old Dodge truck.

"Ignore the mess." He rearranged some books and papers on the seat. "Neatness has never been one of my virtues."

Lily listened to Charlie's cheerful banter as they bounced down the road. He was easy to be with, much like what she had imagined a father or a loving uncle to be. Gentleness lived in Charlie's eyes. His questions seemed genuine, neither threatening or intrusive.

To Lily's surprise, she found herself sharing things she had never told anyone about her fear of rejection and the loneliness that plagued her. Such candor was freeing, but at the same time confusing. Lily wondered where her old feelings of vulnerability had gone.

Charlie turned onto a field, paying no attention to the charred patch of earth where Lily guessed the church had once stood. The old truck rolled past a modest trailer house and continued down a deeply rutted road. He pointed toward the river. "That's where we're setting up chairs. Ah, good, we have help!" Beneath the shade of the cottonwoods, a small group had congregated.

The pastor backed the truck toward the grassy riverbank and threw it into park. He hopped out and opened Lily's door. "I brought a guest," he announced, and made the introductions.

Shyness overshadowed Lily, but the people welcomed her warmly. Together they unloaded chairs and placed them in the shade as others arrived.

From beneath an old cottonwood tree, Lily watched this curious lot. Her heart stirred as she observed children running through the tall grass, giggling. Adults chatted and fondly embraced one another.

Pastor Charlie raised his hands and smiled. "This is the day that the Lord has made," he said. "Let's rejoice and be glad in it!"

Joy shined on all the people's faces. Lily longed to know such peace. Whoever had burned the building had been unable to break their spirits.

—⁓—

Friday, July 7

On the hillside above the mobile home, Peter passed the afternoon watching the tiny anthills at his feet. He slipped a book of matches from his pocket and flicked a flame upon the sandy mound. The tiny creatures scurried about. It reminded him of his own life and all the times when he'd been burned.

Peter's leg throbbed. The pain had worsened and he needed his medication. With a grimace, he climbed to his feet, propped the crutches under his arm, and headed back to the trailer.

Charlie's truck sat in the driveway. Peter wondered how he had missed the man's arrival. All afternoon cars had come and gone as the congregation gathered at the river. Peter had watched them, joining hands and singing their pathetic songs. "Christians," he hissed.

Each swing of the crutch brought Peter one step closer to relief. He summoned strength, struggled up the rickety steps, and hobbled inside.

The living room was empty, allowing Peter to slip down the hallway to his room unnoticed.

He pushed his door open with a crutch.

Pastor Waits was standing near the foot of his bed. "What are you doing in here?"

The old man held a piece of paper. "I was gathering clothes for a load of laundry and I found this."

Peter's face felt hot. "You had no right to go through my things."

"I though it was just a crumpled piece of scrap paper." Charlie stared at the snapshot. He blinked as if trying to process what he'd found. "It's a photograph of me, taken many years ago at a pow-wow. Where did you get it?"

Peter felt his jaw muscles tense. "My mother gave it to me." He watched the color drain from Charlie's face.

The old man sat on the edge of the bed, his dark eyes pooled with tears.

"That's right," Peter said. "I'm your son!"

CHAPTER 29

I slept, and dreamed that life was Beauty;
I woke, and found that life was Duty.
Ellen Hooper

Wyoming
Saturday, July 8

"It's been a while since I've had lunch at the Fischer Creek Café," Anna said as Addison pulled a chair from the table and offered her a seat.

"I apologize for bringing you to this little greasy spoon." He checked his watch. "If I didn't have a meeting with Randolph Harrington, I would have taken you to a restaurant with a more sophisticated menu."

"I like this place," Anna said. "Mom-and-pop restaurants are a little piece of Americana."

"That's a polite way of looking at it." Addison cast a somber glance her way. "I suppose you're wondering why I arranged this little date."

Anna studied the menu. "Since when do you need

a reason for having lunch with an old friend?"

Addison's mouth formed a pout. "I've been very worried about you, my dear."

Behind the menu, Anna contemplated telling her old friend that she found his condescending tone offensive. She bit her tongue.

"Your loss has been difficult, I know, but work will help you get on with your life. I'm sure your father would want you to carry on."

Anna closed the menu. "It's only been a few weeks," she reminded Addison.

"Yes, of course, my dear." His brow creased with pity.

A bald-headed man appeared to take their order and Anna ordered a bowl of vegetable soup.

The man scribbled on his pad. "That all you want?"

"I'm not very hungry," Anna said. "But a cup of herb tea would be nice—any kind will do."

"Make it two cups of tea," Addison said, "but I prefer Red Zinger."

A stout man in a leather vest lumbered past their table and straddled a stool at the counter. "Morning, Milo," he said. "How's business?"

"It's been better," Milo grumbled.

Addison drummed his fingers on the table. "I'd like a French dip. No butter on the bread. And if there's fat on the broth, please have it skimmed."

Milo's lips tightened. "One French dip," he said, emphasizing the last word. He left, but promptly returned with a selection of herb teas and two pots of hot water.

Addison bobbed a bag of Red Zinger in his cup. "Are you aware that Gabor Gagne will be a guest at the Harrington's dinner party?"

Anna shook her head.

"I understand he's flying in this week, staying as their guest until the wilderness dedication." Addison took a loud sip of tea. "What an honor—the founder of the Endangered Earth Alliance, here! I hear you met him in Geneva. Tell me—what's he like?"

"He seemed like a nice man," Anna said without enthusiasm.

Addison frowned. "Anna, dear, nothing excites you anymore. Could be depression, you know. Maybe you should see a doctor."

Silence settled over the table. Maybe Addison was right. Ever since William Vonsetter's telephone call, she had been restless and ill at ease.

When the food arrived, Anna forced herself to eat the bland-tasting soup.

Addison laid the knife on the edge of his plate and lowered his voice. "Do you remember Cassandra Fischer, the woman we visited at the Broken Arrow Ranch?"

"Yes. She just lost her father."

The silver-haired man held his finger to his lips. "The couple who owns this café are Cassandra's in-laws," he whispered, then glanced around to make sure he had not been overheard. "Their son, Reuben, is a suspect in the rancher's murder. I understand he's hiding out somewhere up in the mountains."

"Really," Anna said, "Big place to hide."

"Quite." Addison rubbed his smooth face. "Where was I going with this? Oh yes—Cassandra accompanied me to the Pristine Valley Nature Coalition meeting—the one you weren't up to attending." He gave Anna a brief disapproving glance. "She has agreed to donate a large sum of money when the estate is settled."

"That seems pretty sudden," Anna said. "I mean, her life has been turned upside down. Her decisions might not be very sound. Maybe you should give her a little time."

"Nonsense," Addison retorted. "She's thrilled to find a group that supports her efforts to stop logging." He dipped his sandwich in a small bowl of beef broth, and took a bite. "We've planted some shiny little helpers. I think Cassandra will be very pleased." He winked mischievously and dabbed at his lips with a paper napkin.

Before Anna could respond, a ruckus erupted near the front of the café. All heads turned toward an angry patron. He slapped his palms on the counter. "Who's in charge of that gas pump out there?" he yelled.

Milo blinked nervously. "That'd be me."

"Well, my mechanic says there was sugar in the gas tank," he snarled. "I bought it here!"

"There has to be some mistake."

"I demand that you pay for the damages!" The customer pulled a folded piece of paper from his pocket and shoved it into the bald man's hand. He stomped toward the exit. He jerked open the door and left with a slam that made the walls tremble. A hush fell over the room.

A heavyset woman emerged from the kitchen, her round face creased with worry.

The café owner stared at the bill in his hand. He looked up at his customers, who awkwardly turned back to their own business. The buzz of conversation returned to normal.

Across the table from Anna, Addison lifted a cup of tea to his mouth. Behind the rim, she detected a smile as though he was enjoying himself.

At the counter, the owner motioned to the heavyset woman. "Grace, I'm going to town with a gas sample. The pumps will be shut down until I get back."

Anna shifted in her seat and turned back to Addison. His smile had turned into a subtle smirk.

Her old friend was definitely amused. But why?

CHAPTER 30

A secret is your slave when hidden,
but your master when revealed.
Anonymous

Iowa
Saturday, July 8

William Vonsetter sat alone in his camper's tiny kitchenette, staring through a smudged and dusty window. This was the perfect campground. Not like those stuffy places with fancy motor homes. Here, his old Travel Queen camper, with its rounded roof and peeling trim, had hardly raised an eyebrow. The folks at the Gypsy Inn were friendly, but not inquisitive as they took William's money. Just the way he liked it.

His nearest neighbors had rolled in a half hour ago—a school bus disguised with a coat of tan paint. William watched the congregation of aging hippies with detached interest. They sprawled lazily on a little patch of grass, passing around a communal watermelon. On the steps of the bus, a hairy toad of a man sat strumming an out-of-tune guitar. The group seemed relaxed and happy. William's sense of logic scorned such reckless ignorance.

He shifted his eyes to a fifteen-foot trailer that appeared to be a permanent fixture in the campground. Everything about the tiny structure communicated personal boundaries, from the straw bales that buttressed its flimsy walls to the vines that grew unchecked across its roof. Behind a dark window, William could just make out the faint glow of a cigarette. He imagined the occupant studying the endless turnover of transients.

Children ran past, tussling over a wobbly bike. They skipped about in the dusky light on dirty bare feet. William could not relate to kids; could not even recall being one. The idea seemed foreign, almost laughable. It was as though he had been born a man, bursting upon the world with his brilliant, probing mind. Even in college, William was miles above the others. No one understood him, that is, until he met Jeffery Lyons.

"With your brains and my drive, we can change the world," Lyons had said. William grew pensive as his thoughts turned to one particular summer night, long ago. He could still recall the stars. How bright they seemed to shine on the rocky shores of Canaan Island. Perfect setting. Three young friends lulled by the ocean, warmed by the glow of beer and campfire. They had talked into the early morning hours. Not of trite or frivolous things, but complex matters—dangerous matters.

A lifetime ago, William thought.

The beans on the burner started spitting and William rose to turn down the flame. "Should have warned someone," he said, his mouth pinched tight in self-recrimination.

In the cocoon-like camper, William brooded about the fate of Malcolm O'Neil. To say he was sorry would be an understatement. He had once loved Malcolm like a brother. A lump of unbridled emotion swelled in his throat. He loathed himself for the indulgence.

Vonsetter scraped some beans onto his plate. In the growing shadows, he ate in silence. *Things will be different with Anna.*

CHAPTER 31

Be wary then; best safety lies in fear
Shakespeare

Wyoming
Saturday, July 8

Reuben traveled with purpose, drawing upon the evasion techniques he had learned in the Special Forces. He stepped softly on spongy loam and rocky creek beds to avoid leaving tracks behind, moving slowly and steadily so as not to attract attention. Still, he felt uneasy. It was quiet—too quiet. For a day and a half now, he had not heard the sound of a dog. This left two possibilities. Either his pursuers were way off the track, or the dogs had been replaced by something better. Reuben guessed the latter.

He looked up at the glowing silhouette of the mountain. The sun had set. He figured he had another fifteen, maybe twenty minutes of daylight left. If his suspicions were correct, and his trackers were now using heat sensors and night-vision apparatus, traveling after dark would no longer be an advantage.

In the dimming light, Reuben searched for a place to hunker down. He spotted a large rock and moved to its edge. He laid his hand on the surface. It was still warm to the touch, perfect for deflecting heat sensors. He found a small cleft there, barely deep enough for shelter. It would have to do.

Reuben rubbed his arms. The temperature had already dropped a few degrees; it would be cold tonight. He scooped fallen pine needles from beneath a dense stand, stuffed them inside his jacket for insulation and nestled close to the rock.

Darkness covered him like a blanket. He closed his eyes, listening to the mountain: a gentle whoosh of a nearby stream, the rustling of nocturnal creatures. Reuben's stomach growled with hunger and his calf cramped. The handful of grass and meager ration of pine nuts was not enough to fuel his aching muscles.

Reuben pulled his legs close to his body for warmth and rested his head on his knees. He tried to still his fears, but the thoughts kept coming, threatening to bring him to the edge of resignation. Fear was not an option. He shoved aside his uncertainties and faced the facts. Someone had tried to kill him and now he was being tracked. If there was a way out of this mess, he would have to find it himself.

A branch snapped. Reuben's senses came alive. He strained his ears, discerning man—probably more than one. They crept closer, hardly making any noise. Reuben felt blood pumping in his neck. He tensed and stilled his breathing. Instinct prompted him to bolt and run, but he waited.

One soft step and then another. In the darkness, Reuben detected movement. A red glow flashed between his eyes. A laser spotlight. *I'm dead.*

"Reuben Fischer, we've got you in our sights." The voice was low and hostile. "Come out slowly with your hands on your head."

He did as he was told, adrenaline pumping through his veins.

"On the ground," one of the men yelled. "Keep your hands where I can see them."

Reuben pressed his cheek to the dirt and flung his arms straight out from his side. He imagined the gun's red laser on the back of his head. Behind him, metal clanked. Handcuffs. Reuben felt a knee on his back. Fingers closed around his wrists.

Fight, he told himself. *Fight to stay alive.*

With the strength of a condemned man, Reuben bucked the attacker from his back and tackled him to the ground.

"Get him off me," the tracker yelled. The laser light bounced around, trying to zero in on the target. Reuben had his pursuer in a headlock. It would be so easy to immobilize him for good.

Footsteps approached—thrashing through the

bush. Reuben waited until the second man was nearly on top of the scuffle. He released his prisoner and threw his legs to the side, knocking the partner to the ground. The gun flew from his hand and clattered on the rocky forest floor.

Reuben scrambled to his feet and bolted blindly into the darkness. Behind him, the trackers gave chase. Broken branches, footprints, wild movements, body heat . . . nothing mattered now but distance.

Reuben found himself in dense woods, the places usually avoided by those who were mountain savvy. But the only nocturnal predator Reuben feared now was man. He moved downward in the darkness, clamoring over fallen logs and clawing through bramble.

His pursuers were somewhere behind him— closing the gap.

CHAPTER 32

Cast your burden on the Lord,
And He shall sustain you;
Psalm 55:22

Wyoming
Monday, July 10

Grace held the legal-sized envelope in her hand, afraid to open it. The return address was that of a law firm she had never heard of. Something told her it was bad news. Grace peered out the café's window.

Outside, Milo was taping plastic-coated out-of-order signs on all the gas pumps.

The malicious act of pouring sugar in the gas supply was hard for her to fathom, yet there was no other explanation. Somebody had done this awful thing. The thought nearly broke her heart. She shook her head sadly and slipped open the envelope.

Grace brushed a tear from her eye as she scanned the typed words.

". . . compensation in full for the damages incurred by contaminated gas."

"Cadillac Escalade."

". . . owner Randolph Harrington."

The letter ended with a threat. "Failure to comply will result in further legal action."

"What's that?" Milo barked.

Grace whirled around to face her husband. "You startled me."

He snapped his fingers and held out his hand.

Grace's head throbbed as she watched her husband read.

Milo's ears turned pink, then red. "Randolph Harrington is claiming our contaminated gas damaged his fancy car. He's suing us for damages." His hand shook. "So that LA bigwig thinks he can just waltz into our community and push people around with his stable of lawyers."

"His vehicle was damaged," Grace said emphatically.

"Yeah, along with several others. I plan to make things good as soon as I figure out where to come up with the money. I just got the estimate for cleaning the tanks. It's not pretty."

"Did you contact the insurance company?"

Milo ran a dirty hand over his sweaty scalp and sank into a chair. "Not covered. They said the tanks should have been locked up." He leaned forward, laced his fingers together and stared at the floor.

"Honey, we've been through hard times before," Grace said. Her husband's jaw muscles tensed. She wanted to move closer to Milo's side, put her arms around him, and assure him that everything would be all right. But she knew better. One touch, one ill-chosen word, one wrong move might light the fuse of his temper.

Overwhelmed by a sense of helplessness, Grace hurried into the kitchen, but she could not outrun her tears. She searched for comfort among the commonplace reminders of her daily routine. But everything in her world was spinning. *And yet,* she reminded herself, *God is in control.* Outside a spattering of rain blew against the windows. Grace looked toward heaven and cried out for help from her heart. *Please Lord Jesus . . .*

—⟋⟋—

Monday, July 10

Peter's leg felt stronger now—enough to bear his weight. He hobbled into the mobile home's small living room and plopped onto the couch with a grunt. "If it wasn't raining outside, I'd be gone old man."

Charlie never looked up from reading his Bible, but Peter caught saw his brow furrow. He knew the words had met their mark.

"I honestly didn't know. If I'd known about you I would have . . ." Charlie's voice trailed off.

"You'd what?" Peter retorted. Pain welled up within him and escaped as anger. "You're no better than all those social workers who pretended to care. In the end they always gave me back to my mother so I could watch her go off on another bender." He slammed his fist on the coffee table. "She told me you didn't want me."

"Your mother said that?" Charlie blinked his sad brown eyes. "It's not true." He cocked his toward the trailer's dusty window. "Why did you come?" he said softly.

The question opened a floodgate of emotion in Peter—years of hopes and dreams, culminating in the disappointment he now felt. He contemplated telling the old man it was none of his business, but something held him back.

Charlie turned a probing gaze upon him.

"I just wanted a better understanding of my heritage, that's all." Peter clamped his arms across his chest. "But you're the last person I would ask."

"I was raised to embrace the culture and ways of the Crow Nation," Charlie said. "The only thing that has changed is my faith." He lifted a long box from the windowsill and opened it. "I'd like you to have this."

For a minute, Peter just stared at the artifact before him. It was a peace pipe, carved from stone, its slender stem carefully wrapped with beaded leather.

"This belonged to your great-grandfather. He was a Crow chief, a man of great courage. Like you, he witnessed many sorrows." Charlie offered the relic. "Please take it."

Peter accepted the gift and studied it with interest. "You don't want it anymore?"

Charlie smiled. "I've found peace."

Peter snapped the box shut, grabbed his crutches, and struggled to his feet. "Too bad you didn't get some of your ancestor's courage. Maybe you could have found the strength to withstand the white man's God."

"Years ago, I worked on a ranch in Alaska," Charlie said. "There I had an opportunity to watch the salmon swimming upriver. They struggled against the flow with great determination, all for a purpose much greater than themselves." Charlie paused. "It takes great inner strength to resist the currents of this world."

"My whole life testifies against this God of yours," Peter said. "Where was he when I was hungry and alone? Where was he when my mother was lying in the gutter or in some drunk's bed?"

"I believe he was holding you." Tears rolled down the pastor's plump cheeks. "Now, in his mercy, the Lord has brought you back to me . . . Son."

Rage flashed through Peter's soul like a firestorm. "You don't deserve to call me your son."

—ɯ—

Monday, July 10

Reuben heard voices in the distance. And dogs baying. He darted toward the cover of the willows near the river. It was boggy there, and each step he took filled his boots with water. At first, the wet, spongy ground had soothed the blisters that covered his feet. But after running all night, the sores had become raw and painful. Dark clouds roiled in the morning sky. They rumbled and spat out fat drops of rain, turning the willow bark the color of deep amber.

Reuben clawed his way to the center of a patch of thorn bushes, settled into the gelatinous soil and squirmed deeper into the mire. Cold seeped through the fibers of his clothing and into his bones. He slathered mud across his face and hair and braced against the chill. Reuben's fingers grew numb, but that was the least of his concerns.

The dogs began yelping wildly. They had detected his scent. He closed his eyes and waited.

Reuben heard the sound of a chopper's blades overhead. On the ground, angry voices, twigs snapping, and the sound of willows being whacked resurrected memories from Vietnam. He closed his eyes.

The jungle was a deathtrap to be conquered. Bayonet in hand, Reuben and his men marched in unison, striking out against the jungle—knowing that behind each canopy of green, death could await them.

Reuben opened his eyes and watched the team of men spread grid-like through the willows.

"I don't know," one of them said. "The signs pointed this way. Where'd those dogs go?"

The rain came down in sheets, and streams trickled across Reuben's face, washing the mud away.

"This storm doesn't help," another called.

Reuben understood the discouragement in their voices. He knew it all too well.

They wandered onward. Their muted words soon faded. The human grid had passed over his hiding place without detecting his presence. For a moment, Reuben entertained the thought of calling his pursuers, surrendering in utter exhaustion of soul and muscle, but he held back. He waited until he could wait no longer. Narcotic warmth crept through Reuben's flesh, beckoning him to close his eyes and drift away to sleep, but he recognized the beginnings of hypothermia and forced himself to rise.

Slightly disoriented, Reuben stumbled out into the open, heading toward the shelf of the riverbank, where he collapsed. Beneath him, gray mounds of wet river rock, still retaining some of the warmth from that morning's sun, revived him and he climbed to his knees.

He followed the line of a large tree root to a small dirt cavern in the wall of the riverbank. He squeezed his frame through the narrow tunnel. Hammering with his fist at stubborn dirt clods, he pushed himself through to a larger cavern. There he curled into a fetal position and listened to the rain beating upon the rocks.

Exhaustion finally gave way to sleep.

He awoke only once in the night, surrounded by blackness so dense it absorbed him. The sound of the river whirled and slapped at the bank outside. The waters were rising with the rain, threatening to fill the cave, but that didn't matter. It had been days since he had eaten. *Death might be a welcome relief.*

CHAPTER 33

*It takes two to speak the truth
—one to speak, and another to hear.*
Henry David Thoreau

Wyoming
Tuesday, July, 11

Something Addison Lee had said over lunch Saturday gnawed at Anna. *"We've planted some shiny little helpers."* She had heard the phrase before, back in her college days among the reckless crowd she once ran with. It was another name for tree spikes. Anna did not approve of the Machiavellian approach to the environmental movement.

She had seen a photo of the carnage caused when a chainsaw blade touched a hidden spike and kicked back on the logger. It was gruesome, sometimes even fatal. Moreover, it was against the law. As far as she was concerned, such intimidation tactics were tantamount to terrorism.

Now, alone in her little cabin, Anna wrestled with her conscience, trying to convince herself that she had misheard or misunderstood. When the internal struggle was over, Anna knew what she had to do. She grabbed a pen and paper and quickly scribbled a note, addressed the envelope to Cassandra Fischer at the Broken Arrow Ranch and took it to her mailbox. The idea of sending an anonymous letter brought a surge of shame and Anna began to have second thoughts. However, before she could change her mind, the mail truck rattled up the road and settled the matter.

Anna put the whole thing behind her as she returned to the cabin. She threw herself into busywork: washing dishes, cleaning cupboards and dusting trinkets. As the day wore on, her restless mood turned to anxiety. It brought to mind a minor earthquake Anna had once experienced in Yellowstone Park. That morning, long before she'd felt the trembler, Anna had documented the animals' strange behavior. They were anxious without apparent reason. Maybe the ground beneath her own feet was shifting.

Anna sat on the driftwood couch and lifted her father's book of newspaper columns. She opened it on her lap and turned pages, welcoming the diversion. Words and phrases, so uniquely Malcolm, brought a measure of comfort.

Anna flipped another page and her eyes froze when she read the column title: "Fresh Science at the

Global Warming Summit." In the article, Malcolm lauded the ideas of a new stable of young scientists, calling them "cutting edge." A few paragraphs later, he debunked the ravings of William Vonsetter, calling them "stale and affected."

"Affected?" Anna said aloud. Her father had stopped short of calling his old friend insane! Had Vonsetter carried a grudge against Malcolm for publicly castigating him? Anna's skin began to crawl. Would Vonsetter's revenge stop with her father?

She pushed the scrapbook aside and lifted the Dartmouth yearbook. It opened easily to the dog-eared and coffee-stained section that showed her father and Vonsetter posing for the Ecology Club. A feeling of repulsion came over Anna as she realized that the same hands that killed her father might have also touched these pages.

Anna stared at the smiling photo of Malcolm and his Ecology Club friends and realized, for the first time, that she knew little of her father's college years. What had he been like? Who was he back then? She leaned closer and studied the photo: Malcolm, young and impetuous, linking arms with William Vonsetter and another wild and rugged-looking young man.

The noon-day sun streamed through the cabin window, blanketing Anna with warmth. She yawned, rested her head on a throw pillow and drifted off to sleep.

Anna called to Malcolm, but he did not hear. With

youthful ease, he bounded up the side of the mountain like a sheep. At the top, a faceless character called Malcolm's name and urged him onward.

"Wait," Anna cried, but her father hurried on.

On the bright beach he turned and waved. "Happy birthday, little Anna!"

The form of William Vonsetter appeared on the cliff above, his shadow blocking the light.

The phone rang. Anna leapt from the couch, disoriented. Panic shot through her as she groped for the phone. "Hello?"

"I'm in the neighborhood and thought I'd give you a call."

She struggled to connect a face with the voice. Suddenly it came to her. "Gabor Gagne," she blurted. "I heard you were going to be arriving a few days ahead of the wilderness dedication."

"That's right." He sounded pleased. "I'm staying at the Harringtons' guest cottage." There was an awkward pause. "I look forward to seeing you at the dinner party tonight." Gabor cleared his throat. "I'm calling about the job offer. I thought it would be awkward to discuss it at dinner."

"I've given the opportunity a great deal of thought," Anna said. "It's very generous. But it's just not a good time for me. I have obligations with the pending wolf reintroduction. I need to see that through."

"I understand," Gagne responded. "Of course, I'm

disappointed, but I still look forward to your company tonight."

Anna hung up with a sense of relief. With that out of the way, she rolled up her sleeves and headed to her desk to organize the piles of gray wolf data.

When she entered the living room, she stopped short. On the floor near the couch, the Dartmouth yearbook lay askew, the binding bent backward. It must have fallen from her lap when she rose to answer the phone. But something didn't look right. Near the book's binding, a patch of sunlight caught a glint of silver. Anna stooped to investigate. Tucked inside a split on the inside cover was a CD. Anna slid it from its hiding place and stared at the crude label. "The Canaan Creed." With a trembling hand, she carried it to her computer, slipped it into the drive, and opened the only file on the disk.

The document was written like a college thesis. It began with thematic expressions of ecological zeal, which Anna found inspiring. Yet as she read further, a sense of unease grew into full-blown discomfort. Subtle threads of duplicity ran through pages of eloquent dissertations on stewardship. One paragraph in particular alarmed Anna.

Fear of eminent human extinction resulting from man-made environmental catastrophes is a powerful motivator. It has the potential to galvanize political masses on a universal scale. Thus, ecological awareness should be taught in such a way as to engender fear. Whether the threat is real or perceived matters not. The goal is to open a floodgate of financial and political capital.

"Pride and presumption," Anna said with disgust. She scrolled to the last page. The author of the rogue document was Jeffery Lyons. The name rang a bell with Anna, but she couldn't quite place it.

The cuckoo clock announced that it was five o'clock. As Anna showered and dressed for the dinner party, questions rolled through her mind. Was this the story Malcolm had been working on? What did it have to do with William Vonsetter? And who was Jeffery Lyons? In her linen dress and sandals, Anna did a quick walk-through of the cabin, checking locks and window latches. First thing tomorrow, she would FedEx this new evidence to Corpizio. Anna slipped the CD into her handbag and opened the door. In the distance, a clap of thunder rumbled across the mountain, and the sky promised rain.

The phone rang, but Anna decided against answering. She needed a break from these four walls. Maybe in the presence of other people, her unease would be put to rest.

—ₘ—

Wyoming
Tuesday evening, July 11

Anna wondered how many bulldozers it took to satisfy Randolph Harrington's pride as she rolled down the long driveway to the log fortress. Quickly, she berated herself for thinking such things. After all, the Randolph Harringtons of this world did great things to further the environmental cause. This billionaire had bankrolled numerous key eco organizations and his media education blitzes had achieved unparalleled success—from the Green Ranger cartoons to the "end of the world as we know it" adult dramas. If anyone had earned a right to squander a few resources and build a mansion in the middle of an elk migration trail, it was Randolph Harrington.

Anna parked her Jeep and tried to clear her head, but all thoughts led back to the rogue document called The Canaan Creed. The implications were huge. If global warming had been packaged with false information—information designed to generate fear and thus revenue, then everything Anna believed in would be in question. Goose bumps rose on her flesh as she grabbed her handbag and headed for the gargantuan double doors.

Inside, a servant took her jacket and presented her to the host, who was surrounded by attentive guests.

Randolph threw his arms wide as though she were

an old friend. "Anna! How wonderful to see you looking so well." He embraced her and discreetly offered his personal sympathies as the other guests pressed in. With a snap of his fingers, Randolph summoned his personal photographer and announced a photo op with Anna O'Neil.

"You are a global celebrity now." Harrington smiled. "Enjoy."

Guests lined up, and before she could protest, Anna was barraged by superficial introductions, smiles, and camera clicks. As the line dwindled, so did Anna's patience.

Finally, she was able to slip away and observe the gathering from a quiet corner of the room. A gangly maid delivered her a chilled glass of Perrier, and for a moment, Anna was content. Across the airy room, she noted the gallery of Russell and Remington paintings—no doubt originals.

Gabor Gagne entered, sending a second ripple of excitement through the room. The founder of the Endangered Earth Alliance spotted Anna and smiled. She raised her glass in acknowledgment.

Addison Lee locked eyes with Anna and fluttered over like a grouse in spring. "Isn't this exciting, my dear? It's like a who's who of the green movement. Everybody who is anybody is here tonight." His gaze swept across a sea of faces and he nodded toward the bar. "See that young man with the sandy hair? He wrote a book about the

Galapagos Islands. It's been his life's work."

Addison clapped his hands together and waved his finger toward a barefoot elfin woman standing near the fireplace. "I can't believe it! That's Fawn Ellis. Remember the woman who lived in a tree for a year?"

Anna swirled her glass of sparkling water.

"I'm dying to meet Gabor Gagne." Addison gave her a pleading look. "Could you?" He clutched Anna's arm and coaxed her across the room.

She made the introductions and then stepped back as Addison assailed Gabor Gagne with a hail of words like wilderness, ecosystem, lawsuit, and connections.

Anna was reminded of something she'd read in The Canaan Creed. Her hand tightened around her purse and the CD it contained. She scanned the room, wondering how many here tonight were masking greed and power-lust with altruism. Suspicion crowded in.

Randolph laid a hand on Anna's shoulder and spun her around. "I insist that you say a few words at the wilderness dedication." He winked. "I'm a very stubborn man, so I'm warning you that 'No' is not an option."

Anna smiled. "I would love to."

Looking pleased, Randolph turned to his other guests. "Let's adjourn to the dining room, shall we?"

Anna took her seat among the honored guests, where she engaged in a spattering of small talk with Randolph's wife, Lily, who seemed self-conscious in her frilly western outfit.

Having pried himself away from Addison's adulations, Gabor Gagne straggled into the dining room and sat beside Anna. He leaned close and whispered, "I requested the same seating arrangement as we had in Geneva. I hope you don't mind."

"With all these interesting people here?" Anna said.

When dinner arrived, Anna concentrated on her vegetables and pushed her elk tenderloin about her plate to make it look as though it had been touched.

Randolph mopped his last bite of meat in some gravy, took a bite, and cocked his head toward Anna. "As soon as the wilderness dedication is out of the way, we must sit down and discuss the proposal for my documentary."

She fidgeted in her seat. "I'm not sure . . ."

"Nonsense." Randolph swilled down some wine and touched a napkin to his mouth. "You're a natural. I submitted video clips from the speech you delivered at the Geneva Summit. My board of directors all agreed with me. 'Star material,' they said." The mogul leaned back in his chair. In the soft light, silver glistened in his raven hair, giving him a greasy look. "Who knows? You might even become an international spokeswoman for eco awareness." The corner of the mogul's mouth drew up in a smirk. "Gabor told me you can be a difficult woman to pin down, but I'm confident you'll make the right decision."

Anna felt like the lad from Jack and the Beanstalk, seated beside the giant, grinding her bones to make his bread. She was grateful when her host redirected his attention to another guest.

Gabor Gagne gave Anna a wink. "It's that headstrong quality of yours that makes you such an asset. You lead; most only follow."

"A lot of sweat has gone into the wolf reintroduction program," Anna said, "and not just mine. I share my success with those who have worked beside me."

"But you're the one who has built a name for yourself," Gabor said.

"Speaking of names," Anna said, desperate to change the subject, "have you ever heard of a man called Jeffery Lyons?"

Gabor considered her question carefully. "Lyons . . . It's vaguely familiar. Why do you ask?"

Anna shrugged. "I read an interesting environmental paper he wrote."

"Lily!" Heads turned as Randolph glowered at his young bride. "What is your salad fork doing on your dinner plate? How many times must I instruct you on etiquette?" He leaned near to his wife and whispered, "Must you act like trailer trash?"

Lily's face flashed with embarrassment. She stammered an apology, then stood and hastily excused herself from the table.

Randolph Harrington sulked through his coffee

and dessert, sucking the life from the dinner party with his brooding silence.

At the first opportunity, Anna rose, tersely thanked her host, and made a gracious departure. She grabbed her handbag and bolted from the mansion like a calf out of the chute. The crisp night air smelled of ozone.

Anna heard a clap of thunder in the distance and felt a raindrop. She climbed into her Jeep and drove from the mountain, feeling lost. The friends and comrades of her past now seemed foreign, even strange to her.

When she reached the valley, Anna pulled into a turnout near the river and sat in the stillness of the night. The dark water moved slowly over the rocks, moonlight catching a shimmer of rain on its surface. For nearly an hour, Anna tried to define her beliefs, but they kept slipping out of reach.

She yawned, unable to deny her exhaustion. Her father used to say, "The difference between hope and despair is often a good night's sleep." Anna started the engine and headed home.

She arrived at her cabin a little before midnight. With key in hand, she flung her backpack over her shoulder, unlocked the door, and flipped on the light.

Anna froze. Her home had been ransacked. Drawers dumped, pillows ripped apart, and papers strewn about. She was stunned. Disbelief gave way to a sickening realization. She was certain that whoever had killed her father was now after her.

Anna raced to her bedroom to stuff clothes and gear into her backpack. Somewhere in the house, a door squeaked and a floorboard groaned under someone's weight. The lights went out.

Anna ran blindly toward the bedroom wall and felt for the window. She struggled to open the rusty window latch.

Footsteps approached.

"No, no," Anna whispered as her fingers fumbled to release the latch. Shoving the window open, she tossed the backpack on the ground and lunged for the opening.

Rough hands grabbed her shoulders, pulling her back. Cold fingers pressed on her neck. Anna tried to twist free, kicking furiously at her assailant. She bit his hand. The enemy yelled and loosened his grip. Anna lunged for the window again, but with vise-like arms, the attacker grasped her midsection, crushing the breath from her lungs. Again, the fingers closed around her neck. Darkness circled. Anna's strength ebbed. *So this is what it's like to die.*

From the shadows, something crashed. Her attacker fell away. Anna gasped for air.

A flurry of fists and guttural sounds ensued as, now, two intruders engaged in a violent struggle. They slammed to the floor; wrestling in the dark she could barely see the shapes.

Life flowed back into Anna's limbs. She clambered to her feet and sprang through the open window.

She sought refuge among the tangled willows near the creek, crouching low beside the babbling brook, her senses sharp. It wasn't safe. They would look for her there.

Anna's arms and legs quivered. She gulped air and tried to be calm. Her fingers throbbed as they clutched her backpack and she thought of the CD she had placed there. The Canaan Creed was like an albatross around her neck, yet ironically, it might be her only hope of getting out of this mess.

She scanned the dusky shadows for movement. Anna caught sight of headlights glinting through the trees. Friend or foe? There was no time to find out. On the other side of the valley lay a star lit mountain silhouette. Up there her survival skills would give her an advantage. Anna bolted into the night and into the open arms of her wilderness.

—⁓—

Maine
Tuesday, July 11

Investigator Corpizio's cell phone chortled. He pulled to the side of the road, pressed the receiver to his ear, and heard the voice of his old partner, Gerri Redding.

"I've been trying to reach you all evening."

"I drove out to Canaan Island to have another look around. No cell signal there. What's up?"

"The phone company just flagged another call to Anna O'Neil's residence in Wyoming. It was made from a phone booth, just like the others."

"Vonsetter?"

"Presumbly. But there's more—a geographic pattern. If you connect the pay phone locations on a map, they point straight to Anna O'Neil. It appears our suspect is on his way to her house. The last call was made from a town called Cedar Ridge."

"We'd better notify the local sheriff."

"Done."

The investigator pressed his foot to the gas pedal. "What about Ms. O'Neil?"

"Either not answering or she's not at home."

I hope, for her sake, it's the latter, Corpizio thought, picking up speed.

CHAPTER 34

Tacitae magis et occultae inimicitiae timendae
sunt quam indicatae et operate
—Enmities which are unspoken and hidden
are more to be feared than those
which are proclaimed and open
Latin-Cicero

Wyoming
Wednesday, July 12

Grace looked out across the Pristine Valley, taking in her daily dose of beauty. The dewy grass sparkled from last night's rain, and the pungent smell of pine rode on a gentle breeze. She smiled at the recollection of her dream, but her eyes filled with tears. Reuben, as a mere boy, ran to her with an offering of wildflowers. "These are for you Mommy!" It had been years since she had been able to hold her firstborn and wrap protective arms around him. Grace sighed wistfully and went inside.

The Fischer Creek Café was quiet, but not for long.

Jody would be there soon. Grace checked her watch, slipped an apron from a hook, and grabbed some breakfast staples from the pantry.

She heard Milo stamp mud from his feet on the wooden porch and whispered a prayer. His mood had been more sour than usual. Grace had sensed it before he rolled out of bed that morning. All night long, her husband had thrashed, snorted, and wrestled with the bedding.

Milo skulked in, wagged his face in both directions, and fixed his sights on light spilling from the pantry door. "Dang it, woman, electricity is money."

Grace ran to the switch while Milo huffed over to the desk and rattled around through the drawers.

"What are you looking for?" she asked, feeling a knot in her stomach.

"The mail—where in the blazes is the mail?"

Grace lifted the newspaper and unearthed a stack of letters.

"How can I pay these bills when you're slapping double portions on all our customers' plates?" he barked. "You need to cut back. There's too much waste as it is."

"Okay, honey," Grace placated.

Milo reached for his wife and gave her a squeeze. "I don't mean to be such a sourpuss," he apologized. "Have I told you lately that you make the best biscuits this side of the Rocky Mountains?"

Grace kissed her husband's cheek. "Thanks."

Jody breezed in, filling the room with chatter.

"Quite a storm last night. We can always use the rain, but I suppose it won't help Dillon." Her face pinched into a scowl. "According to the news, it's still raining up high. I hope the roads aren't muddy and slick. Did I tell you that Cordell went along to help?" Jody crossed her fingers. "I hope Dillon comes down from the mountain with his quota. The lumber company had a talk with him the other day. Said they'd have to break his contract if he didn't produce."

Grace nodded sympathetically to her daughter-in-law as Milo disappeared into the storage room.

"What's wrong with him?" Jody whispered.

"He didn't sleep well last night." *Or the night before.* Her husband's sallow skin and dark circles spoke volumes. "Milo just needs a little peace," she said. But her optimism fell flat when the Badland boys walked in.

Juke, the tall one, sauntered through the door, sniffing the air like a hound dog. "Where's yer husband?"

Grace heard Milo banging around in the storage room. "He's busy right now."

Juke ran long, greasy fingers through stringy hair and took a step toward the storage room. "Ol' Milo always has time for friends." He rapped his knuckles on the doorframe. "Hey, Fischer."

Milo poked his shiny head through the door. "What?"

"Come on out and be sociable." Juke turned to Jody, signaled for some service, and plopped down at a table with the other two Badland boys.

Jody slopped coffee in his cup and dropped menus on the table.

Juke summoned Milo with his long, bony finger. "Word's out," he rumbled, low and cryptic. "Everybody knows the government is trying to run you off."

From behind the counter, Grace cleaned the coffee maker while keeping an anxious eye on the exchange.

Juke slid a mangled toothpick from his pocket, propped it on his tongue, and awaited Milo's response.

Grace felt light headed with worry. Between Reuben's disappearance, Dillon's troubles, money woes, and legal troubles, this dose of paranoia might be more than her husband could take.

Milo's jaw muscle clenched, then relaxed, and clenched again, as it always did when he was angry. "I don't have time for this nonsense!" He turned on his heels and stomped away.

"Suit yourself," the young man grumbled. "But don't say I didn't warn ya."

A coffee pot slipped through Grace's fingers and shattered at her feet. Jody hurried over to help her mother-in-law.

"Thank you, honey." Grace grabbed a dishtowel and dried sweat from her palms. Her stomach hurt from stress and the tension in her neck was building into a nasty headache. *Be strong,* she told herself. Nevertheless, Grace felt weak. *Lord, help me.* A measure of peace settled around her, but deep down, something told Grace the worst was yet to come.

—⚏—

Wednesday, July 12

Dillon hoisted the log into the trailer. He lifted his John Deere cap and wiped the sweat from his brow. "Should we call it a day?"

Cordell took a swig of Coke and considered the question. He looked back at the loaded trailer. "I think we've got room for a few more trees."

Dillon eyed his nephew. "Think so?" Dillon was tired and his foot throbbed. But one more log wouldn't hurt. Hard work helped take his mind off things: mounting bills, his brother Reuben, and all the people bent on destroying his livelihood. "I'm game if you are."

A few minutes later, the two men were grinding along Cutter Creek in Dillon's salvaged truck. He shifted the transmission into low gear, carefully rocked the tires over some deep ruts, and pulled over to the edge of the meadow. "Daylight's burning," he said, rolling to a stop. He stomped on the emergency brake, hopped out, and pulled the chainsaw from the truck bed. "You ever worked one of these?"

Cordell's face lit up. "Really? You're gonna let me do it this time?"

Dillon poured gasoline and oil into the power tool,

fired it up, and handed it to his nephew. He pointed to a dead-standing tree and stood back to watch.

The loud whine of the motor drowned out Cordell's words, but his smile said it all. The tree cracked and toppled to the ground.

"You're doing a great job," Dillon yelled as the teenager cut the tree into manageable lengths.

Cordell laid the chainsaw on the road to idle while he inspected his work. "One more, Uncle Dillon?"

"Want me to run the chainsaw?"

"Are you kidding?" Cordell scooped the tool from the ground. "I can handle it."

Dillon smiled. "Just like your father." Whenever there was work to be done, Reuben was the last to hang his hat on the peg.

Cordell revved up the chainsaw to a high whine and laid the blade to a marked tree. The late-afternoon sun was sinking fast. There would be just enough light to get this last tree cut and loaded and make it down from the mountain before dark. Dillon took a pull from a water jug, slipped on his sawdust-covered gloves, and started toward his nephew.

From the corner of his eye, Dillon saw the Broken Arrow Ranch vehicle bouncing across the meadow. "What in the world?" He squinted into the setting sun. This time Cassandra had gone too far.

Behind Dillon, the shrill sound of metal on metal assaulted the air, followed by a dull thump. Dillon turned to see Cordell stagger backward, the chainsaw at his feet. A look of shock covered the teenager's face. He opened his mouth, but only a strange guttural sound gurgled from his lips. Cordell's chest sprouted blood. He sank to the ground. Dillon raced to his side.

The reality of the situation suddenly registered in his mind. Someone had driven a nail pike into the tree!

The ranch vehicle roared closer and Cassandra spilled out, clutching a letter in her hand. "I'm too late," she screamed and dropped to her knees on the blood-soaked ground. Cordell's eyes were wide with fear as his mother cupped his face. "Baby? Baby!"

"It hurts," he moaned, his words escaping in a weak thread.

"I'm sorry. I'm so sorry," Cassandra sobbed. "I got a letter in the mail warning me about tree spiking. I didn't know they would resort to terrorism. I swear, I didn't know."

Dillon grasped her arm. "We've got to get him down from the mountain. He's losing blood fast." He lifted Cassandra's hand and placed it on the gaping wound. Beneath her fingers, blood coursed with each beat of her son's heart. "Apply pressure," Dillon ordered. "Don't let go, even when I lift him. Do you understand?" The boy's mother nodded as if in a trance.

Dillon threw open the rear door of the Suburban and carefully lifted his nephew into the back. Cassandra, her hand still firmly on the wound, climbed in beside Cordell.

Dillon leapt into the driver's seat, cranked the key, and headed for town.

With every rut and bump, the boy cried out in pain while his mother chanted, "I'm sorry," over and over again.

—ᙡᙡ—

Wednesday, July 12

Reuben lay motionless in the cramped dirt hovel. Outside, he could hear the swollen river tumbling over river rocks and small boulders. Closer still was the steady drip, drip, drips as raindrops fell into a nearby puddle. The sound mocked Reuben's thirst. It had been days since he had taken nourishment, and the previous cold, damp night had leached more strength from his already weakened flesh.

The burrow barely afforded enough room for Reuben to spread out. His muscles were stiff and cramped from their unnatural positions. A sense of hopelessness overpowered him, warring against the will to survive.

Reuben shut his eyes and tried to drift away. When he opened them again, a ray of golden sunlight was streaming into his hiding place, signaling the storm's retreat. He lifted his hand to the mote-filled light. He thought about how good it would feel to crawl from this hole and allow the warm sun to soothe his bone-chilled body, but he dared not. The water had risen during the night. Once, it had come perilously close to flushing him from his burrow. Yet the rain-gorged river had been a godsend, cleansing the bank of any scent or sign that he had been there.

For the time being, he was safe. Yet his profound weakness was a signal of another problem—hunger. He needed to regain his strength, but he couldn't risk being seen in broad daylight.

Too tired to reason, Reuben's thoughts turned to a quote he had once read: "I have been driven many times to my knees by the overwhelming conviction that I had nowhere else to go." Reuben found comfort in those words, knowing that the man who had written them, Abraham Lincoln, had once carried the weight of a divided and battered nation on his shoulders.

His thoughts shifted to his Vietnam days. There, Reuben had drawn close to God, only to slip away by tiny measures with each passing year since. Now he, like Lincoln, was being driven back to his knees.

"Lord, I don't know why any of this has happened or what you want from me. But I pray that somehow you'll bring me through." He whispered his regrets to God—regrets of the past twenty years.

In the solitude of the cavern, Reuben realized that he had become emotionally inaccessible to those around him. He wept for the years he had wasted apart from God. He wept for his failures as a husband and father. In his mind's eye, he visualized his family. He saw Cassandra, with the innocence and softness she had once carried as a new bride, before the seeds of petty jealousies and bitterness sprouted. He saw Cordell as the tiny cowboy, hip deep in boots and dwarfed beneath his daddy's Stetson hat.

The memories rolled like crashing waves. He had let his family down. In grief and sorrow, Reuben cried out to God like never before.

A peaceful feeling enveloped him. Was it real? Or just delirium brought on by thirst and hunger? Was death closing in? It didn't seem to matter. In the stillness of his hiding place, he rested. And for the first time in days, he felt a renewed surge of hope.

An odd noise stole the silence. It was the sound of splashing, as if a hand had slapped the surface of a puddle. He heard it again. Was it an intruder? Reuben strained his ear to listen, but heard nothing else. No footsteps crunching on river rock—nothing.

It took every centimeter of space to turn his frame around in the cramped quarters. In the process, he loosed a hanging dirt clod, and it crumbled on his head. Reuben brushed it off and slowly inched his torso through the cave's narrow entrance. Among the gnarled and twisted tree roots, a puddle had filled with river water from the deluge in the night. In it were three brook trout.

If there had ever been even a seed of doubt in Reuben's mind about the existence of God, in that moment it disappeared. He plucked one of the fish from the puddle and thanked the Lord. Sushi had never tasted better.

CHAPTER 35

Love . . . bears all things, believes all things,
hopes all things, endures all things.
1 Corinthians 13:7

Wyoming
Wednesday, July 12

By the time Grace and her husband arrived at the hospital, Cordell was already in surgery. Dillon ushered his parents into a small waiting room. In a corner chair, Cassandra sat like a forlorn child, rocking slowly, rhythmically, her face buried in her arms.

Grace reached out to her daughter-in-law and touched her shoulders, which quaked softly as she cried. "Cassie, honey . . ."

Cassandra lifted a mottled face. "Oh, Grace," she moaned. "What have I done?"

The older woman opened her ample arms to enfold her daughter-in-law. "Everything's going to be all right," she whispered, stroking Cassandra's tangled hair.

Milo poured coffee into a Styrofoam cup and turned to Dillon. "What happened up there?"

"It was intentional, Dad."

Grace studied her youngest son, whose plaid shirt was stained with caked blood.

"What do you mean?" Milo pressed.

Dillon's face stiffened with anger. "Somebody drove a spike in the tree."

Milo stared at his son. A long, dark silence followed.

Grace felt a growing sense of dread as she watched her husband seethe like a thunderhead.

A doctor in green scrubs appeared in the doorway. All eyes shifted his way.

Cassandra reached for her mother-in-law's hand. Grace felt her tremble as the doctor approached.

"Mrs. Fischer." He smiled slightly. Cassandra's features seemed frozen with fear. "Your son has been stabilized. He lost a lot of blood, but we believe he is going to be all right. There may be some nerve damage. We'll know more when he wakes up."

"Oh, thank God!" Cassandra hugged Grace. "Thank God." Her body relaxed and she turned to her in-laws. "I hope all of you can stay. I know Cordell would be happy to see you when he wakes up."

Through grateful tears, Grace watched her daughter-in-law cross the room to where Dillon stood. Cassandra curled her fingers around his arm. "Thank you for giving my son back to me."

CHAPTER 36

Only the actions of the just
Smell sweet and blossom in their dust.
James Shirley

Maine
Wednesday, July 12

"I've booked a flight to Wyoming," Corpizio announced when Gerri walked into his office.

"That doesn't surprise me. Any new developments?"

The investigator shook his head. "No sign of Ms. O'Neil."

"At least they've got Vonsetter in custody. Is he talking?"

Corpizio laced his fingers behind his course head of hair. "He just keeps rambling on—claims he rescued Anna from some lions."

"Yeah, and tigers and bears, I'm sure," Gerri retorted. "Just like he rescued her father and this poor sod in Arizona." She tossed a file onto the desk in front of her old partner. "The sheriff in Phoenix is interested in talking to William Vonsetter as soon as you're finished with him."

Corpizio leaned over the file. "About what?"

"A few years back, a body was found in an apartment leased to William Vonsetter."

Corpizio stared at Gerri. "Who was the victim?"

She raised her shoulders in a shrug. "The dead man's identity is still a mystery."

Corpizio sat straight. "I thought Vonsetter was clean."

"Never trust a rap sheet, I always say. Our mad scientist was never actually charged with a crime, not even brought in for questioning."

"So, no fingerprints, no warrant issued, no arrest, and therefore, no national record."

"Bingo."

He glanced at the clock on the wall and stood. "I've got a plane to catch."

—❧—

Wyoming
Wednesday, July 12

In the dusty stream of light that filtered into the hovel, Reuben watched a pine beetle slowly march up the dirt wall. It crawled halfway, lost its footing, fell, then started again. Reuben cheered the tiny creature on, saddened when it landed on its back. The bug flailed helplessly. Reuben scooped the tiny insect into his calloused hand, placed it near the cave's opening, and watched it crawl to a sunlit rock. It lingered there, oblivious to hungry birds and the river currents that swirled nearby. Free, yet blissfully ignorant of the dangers—the same place Reuben had been a few weeks ago. Now it all came down to survival.

He felt hungry again and his skin was chilled and clammy from the damp. He could not stay in this cramped hovel much longer. Already, his knotted muscles were beginning to atrophy, but to risk leaving now seemed foolish. The dogs would pick up his scent, and he would be hunted again like an animal.

A crunching sound met his ear. With the self-control of a seasoned soldier, Reuben's senses were at the ready. Footsteps fumbled on the river rock, faint, yet coming closer, until they were almost upon his hiding place. The visitor cleared his throat—probably a man— not more that a few yards away.

Reuben closed his eyes, imagining the movements on the other side of the embankment. The person settled down for a rest and threw a pebble or two. Soon, the movement grew minimal and Reuben inched toward the opening to assess the situation. There, sleeping peacefully, was a man, probably in his early thirties, slim, muscular, and potentially deadly. Unlike the other trackers, he wore a gray uniform.

Beside him, a backpack lay open, revealing the remnants of a half-eaten sandwich. Reuben stretched his body around the gnarl of roots and reached inside the pack.

The young man coughed, shifted. Reuben froze until the rhythmic breathing resumed. He closed his fingers around the sandwich and carefully pulled it toward him.

Reuben spotted the shiny handle of a gun poking out from beneath the lunch sack. It was similar to the one he sometimes carried in the mountains as a protection against bears.

It would be easy to slide the weapon from its holster and shoot the enemy while he lay sleeping. In the jungles of Nam, he had seen it done more than once. Young American soldiers slain by Viet Cong as they slept. It was an unwelcome and cruel memory, one that had surfaced many times over the years to rob Reuben of sleep.

His fingers inched closer to the holster. Even if the gunfire alerted others, he rationalized, the weapon might just be his ticket to freedom. One clean shot, that's all it would take.

He looked at the young man, whose youthful lips curled into a slight smile. What was he dreaming?, Reuben wondered, of a wife, maybe kids?

He moved his fingers away from the gun and took the sandwich instead. It went down fast.

The minutes ticked by in silence. The sound of a branch breaking woke the man with a start. His leg shot forward, launching a couple of river rocks from their resting place. "Stop!" he yelled.

Reuben felt a thud on the dirt wall, as if the man had banged his head on the other side. Dust rained down inside the hovel.

"Come out with your hands up or I'll shoot!"

This is it, Reuben thought. With resignation, he inched toward the opening. Sunlight streaked into his weakened eyes.

"Hey, put that thing down!" called a woman's voice.

The man had not been talking to Reuben after all! As his eyes adjusted to the light, he saw a young woman just across the river, moving closer, with arms raised high.

Her face seemed familiar. Reuben was sure he had seen her around, though he didn't know the woman's name. She looked more angry than frightened.

"I'm sorry, Miss." The man lowered his pistol. "I thought you were someone else."

"Do you always go around scaring hikers?" she snapped.

"Did you know there's a dangerous fugitive in this area?"

"No."

"I think it would be best if you leave."

The woman stepped on a tree that had fallen across

the river. With arms extended for balance, she stepped carefully to the other side.

The man slid his pistol back into the holster and offered her a hand. She ignored the gesture and hopped down from the makeshift bridge unaided. "Are you ordering me to go?" she asked with a defiant tone.

"No, ma'am, I'm not authorized to do that."

"What are you, Forest Service?"

"I'm from the Special Law Enforcement Division," he said defensively. "I strongly advise you to turn back now, ma'am. This man is very dangerous."

"I'm more worried about guys like you packing guns than I am about some fugitive. What did he do, anyway?"

"He is a murder suspect—wanted for questioning."

Reuben's heart sank with the confirmation of what he had feared. Duke was dead. He shifted slightly, and a clod of dirt gave way, pelting his eye. It stung, but he dared not make any sudden moves to wipe it away.

Reuben's vision cleared, and he was startled to see the young woman staring directly at him. She quickly looked away. "You've got me spooked," she said to the lawman. "Would you mind walking me to the trail?"

"No problem, ma'am."

Reuben listened until the small talk faded away. She had seen him, he was sure of that. Why hadn't she given him away? There was no time to wonder about her motives. He squeezed through the opening of the burrow and scooted along the edge of the river. He dropped into the water, staying close to its grassy overhang.

Just around the bend, Reuben knew the waters narrowed through a canyon and tumbled into a short, but violent, set of rapids. Just beyond that, the river spilled into a lazy, wide meander through an open basin. This worried Reuben more than the rapids did. There he would be a sitting duck.

—∿∿—

Wyoming
Wednesday July 12

As Anna backtracked through the forest, she recalled the fugitive's dirty face, peeking out from the tree-root hovel, his clueless tracker only a few yards away. It was comical, really, and if her own situation had not been so sobering, Anna would have pointed the man out and enjoyed a good laugh from it. But things had changed—oh, how they had changed!

Perhaps she and this fugitive could help each other.

It had taken Anna more than an hour to shake the law-enforcement officer. To make matters worse, she got herself rimmed in by cliffs as she was trying to find her way back to the hiding place.

As she approached the root-bound cave, she wondered if he'd stayed. She cautiously drew near and knelt next to the opening. "Hello?" She peered into the black hole. "Is anyone there?" Getting no response, she squeezed halfway through the opening, marveling that any man could fit through it.

The cave was abandoned. She backed out, brushed the dirt from her clothes, and looked around, wondering where she would go to avoid detection if she were in his position. Neither the hillside to the right of the river nor the one to the left afforded enough cover. The direction from which she had come was not an option, for that was the way the lawman had gone.

Anna decided the river was the best choice. She waded along the bank, discerning subtle signs as she went—a possible handprint in the mud, a broken piece of dirt bank, moss scraped from a rock. The water deepened. The current grew strong. Anna planted her feet firmly as the chilly waters swirled around her waist.

She lifted the pack above her head and looked around for an alternate route. The current tugged on her legs, and a rock rolled beneath her shoe. Anna struggled for footing on the mossy bottom, but lost her balance. In an instant, the river snatched the backpack from her hand.

The Canaan Creed CD!

Anna lunged for the pack as it tumbled down the river, but it bobbed just out of reach.

Around the bend, the sound of water tumbled and hissed, bringing a wave of fear. She paddled furiously for the shore. The river coursed deep, swallowing her beneath the surface and spitting her out. Anna gasped for air and went under again.

The river roared like a monster, scraping and slamming Anna into rocks and snags. Finally, utterly exhausted, she could fight the powerful currents no longer. Anna gave in to the raging torrent and felt her limp body roll over the waves like a rag doll. Down river, the waters descended into a cascading blur of white, which split around a fallen tree.

Anna rallied to grab a branch as the current thrust her closer to the trunk. She positioned herself as best she could, but an eddy spun her body backward and slammed her against the downed tree. A stabbing pain shot through Anna's side. She looked down. Just above her hip, a branch protruded through her gray fleece jacket. A crimson stain wicked across the garment and trickled into the foamy water. She had been impaled!

Anna tried to free herself, but the force of the current pushed against her like a bully. Thoughts of death crawled across her battered flesh. *Not like this.*

She looked skyward, beyond the canyon walls. The nearest trail was miles away. It would be useless to scream. Who would hear?

Anna tried to break the waterlogged skewer, but it would not give. Blood streamed into the river. "God," Anna cried out, mentally adding, *if there is a God,* "I need help!"

Just then, a bearded man emerged from behind a boulder and moved to the river's edge. It was the fugitive from the cave.

CHAPTER 37

Method is good in all things. Order governs the world.
The Devil is the author of confusion.
Jonathan Swift

Wyoming
Thursday, July 13

Corpizio watched from the window seat as the small commuter plane circled the tiny Wyoming airport and swooped down upon Cedar Ridge. The investigator disembarked on the tarmac with the other passengers: an elderly gentleman, four women, and a child. Corpizio followed them to the gate.

The local sheriff waited just inside the airport. He tipped a seasoned cowboy hat. "You must be from the Maine State Police." The man pumped Corpizio's hand. "I'm Sheriff Luther Hodge. Most folk call me Hodge."

The square built sheriff ushered the newcomer to a squad car.

"Have there been any new developments?"

Corpizio asked as the sheriff pulled onto the highway.

"Still no sign of the O'Neil woman."

"What about Vonsetter?"

"That man loves to talk, I'll say that much." The sheriff chuckled. "Can't make much out of his ramblings, but there sure are a lot of interested listeners."

"What do you mean?"

"You're not our only visitor." Up ahead, the highway merged into Cedar Ridge's Main Street and the sheriff braked for a stoplight. "Two feds showed up this morning to have a little chat with our suspect."

"What's their interest?"

The sheriff lifted the brim of his cowboy hat and scratched his head. "I don't rightly know. Those high-ridin' city boys told me to take a long coffee break." He pulled into a reserved parking spot. The Sheriff escorted Corpizio through the double glass doors of the county law-enforcement office.

The jail was a small concrete building with a short hallway flanked by offices. The laid-back dispatcher looked up when her boss appeared, gave him a bored yawn, and returned her attentions to a paperback book.

Sheriff Hodge offered Corpizio a cup of coffee and he accepted. "I think the feds are with Vonsetter now. At least they were when I left. Probably won't take too kindly to being disturbed."

Corpizio took a sip of stout black coffee and set his mug on a wobbly table. "What can you tell me about Ms.

O'Neil's cabin?"

The sheriff chortled. "The government boys have deemed that off limits too. They've cordoned it off and their forensic experts are dusting the place." He whistled through his stained teeth. "When I saw the cabin, it was ransacked, as if somebody was pretty interested in finding something. We found Vonsetter crouching in a thicket of lilac bushes beside the house—claimed he'd been chasing a lion. The guy's half a bubble off level if you ask me."

"Were there signs of violence?"

"It looked like there'd been a struggle in the bedroom and Vonsetter was roughed up pretty good. That O'Neil woman must have put up a good fight."

Down a short corridor, a door opened and a man in a black suit emerged. "Does this town have any carryout?"

Sheriff Hodges smirked. "Yeah, all our fine restaurants let you carry food out, but you have to go get it yourself."

The government man did not appear humored.

"This is Investigator Jay Corpizio from the Maine State Police," the sheriff said. "He's here to question our suspect in connection with a couple of murders up his way."

The man thrust out his hand. "Greg Iverson. FBI."

"I'm investigating the murders of Malcolm O'Neil and one of our deputies," Corpizio said.

"Would you care to join us?" The agent pointed the way.

"Hey, don't you boys worry about me," the sheriff quipped. "I'll be out checkin' the roads for pot holes."

In a sterile room with an institutional table and some folding chairs, the FBI man introduced Corpizio to his partner, a crew-cut military type named Chaz.

"Sit down," Agent Iverson said.

Corpizio did as he was told.

"We know all about the murder of Malcolm O'Neil," Iverson said. "And the unfortunate death of the deputy."

Corpizio laced his fingers together and tried not to look surprised. "What else do you know?"

"That William Vonsetter didn't kill them," Agent Chaz interjected.

Corpizio looked at the government men, his eyes narrowed. "We've got a profile on Vonsetter and . . ."

Iverson held up his hand. "A few months ago, Malcolm O'Neil contacted us about a man named Jeffery Lyons."

"I know that name," Corpizio said. "The Dartmouth Ecology Club."

"That's right. But I'd wager that's as far as you got. Even the FBI couldn't pull up anything on the guy. It was as if he'd dropped into a black hole. Then one day Malcolm O'Neil called us. He said Jeffery Lyons was living under an assumed identity and was involved in some kind of grand-scale fraud. O'Neil planned to contact us as soon as he got the proof—that was the last time we heard from him."

Corpizio absorbed the information. "So where does Vonsetter come in?"

"He had the proof. A document called The Canaan Creed—some kind of ecology manifesto written by the elusive Jeffery Lyons."

"Have you seen it?"

Agent Chaz raised an eyebrow and exchanged an inquisitive look with his partner, who nodded. Chaz turned back to Corpizio. "Vonsetter says he sent it to Anna O'Neil. He claims, his conscious started to bother him. He was worried about her and decided to head her way. The night she disappeared, Vonsetter said he surprised Jeffery Lyons in the process of attacking Ms. O'Neil. He intervened and the two men went to blows."

Agent Iverson unscrewed the cap from a bottle of water. "Vonsetter must have been knocked out. When he came to, Lyons and O'Neil were both gone. She may have fled to the mountains." He took a drink. "We contacted the Game and Fish and Forest Service people. They said one of their men spotted a woman who fits her description."

Corpizio stood. "Does Vonsetter know where to find Lyons?"

"We could wrap this thing up in a hurry if he did," Agent Iverson said.

"I want to talk to him."

"Suit yourself." Chaz showed him down the hall to the holding room.

Vonsetter sat at a table, knees nervously banging

together, fingers drumming on his thighs, eyes wide and intense. "I didn't do it," he announced. "I didn't kill Malcolm. Not directly anyway."

Corpizio pulled a chair in front of the suspect. "What do you mean?"

The scientist's eyes darted around the room. "When Malcolm asked me about The Canaan Creed, I knew there was going to be trouble, just like before." The man's lanky frame hunched over the table and he peered at Corpizio from beneath bushy eyebrows.

"Tell me more about this Canaan Creed."

"Malcolm and I used to be friends. But Jeffery changed everything." Vonsetter studied an age spot on the back of his hand.

"How?"

"The Canaan Creed. It was Jeffery's thesis. He came up with it one weekend during a camping trip."

"Let me guess," Corpizio said. "Canaan Island?"

"A 'social experiment,' Jeffery called it." When he asked me to type it up, I kept a copy. Had it kicking around for years. Didn't give it any thought until the global warming summit."

"What made you think of it then?" Corpizio asked.

"The pattern! It all fit."

"Did you discuss this with anyone?"

Vonsetter's eyes clouded. "The scientific community was a sham. There were exceptions, though. Like Steven Hoffman." He paused. "He was heavy into superconductors—maybe you've heard of him."

Corpizio shook his head. "I'm afraid I don't run in those circles."

"After Hoffman read Lyons's thesis, he brought his concerns to some high-level people he knew." A look of remorse passed across Vonsetter's face. "Don't know who Hoffman talked to. But not long after, the police found his body in my apartment. Mutilated almost beyond recognition." The scientist pinched the bridge of his nose and squeezed his eyes shut. "I can still see it in my head," he lamented. He looked sharply at Investigator Corpizio. "Been on the run ever since."

"What's in the document?"

Vonsetter folded his arms across his chest and shook his head. "Knowledge is leverage. I need to know who I can trust." A childlike smile spread across the old man's lips and morphed into a grin. "I have copies, though."

"Where?"

Vonsetter focused on a hangnail. He bit it off.

"Did you give a copy to Anna O'Neil?"

"People listen to her," Vonsetter said eagerly. "She's a perfect vehicle for justice."

If she lives long enough, Corpizio thought.

CHAPTER 38

I fear to love thee sweet
because love's the ambassador of loss.
Francis Thompson

Wyoming
Thursday, July 13

Lily peered into the bathroom mirror. Her face was puffy from crying—another sign of weakness, deplorable by her husband's standards. She couldn't help but wonder if the marriage had been a mistake. Randolph used to gaze at her as he would a painting in a gallery. That had been tolerable. But ever since the dinner party, he seemed to look upon her with a mixture of disgust and embarrassment. Another swell of tears surfaced.

She splashed cold water on her face, dusted her cheeks with powder and ventured downstairs. Randolph was on the phone, as usual. Near the window, Gabor Gagne stood with a glass of tomato juice in hand.

Lily noticed a bandage on his brow as he turned

her way. "What happened?"

"A little riding accident," he said with a brush of his free hand. "I wanted the horse to go across a creek, but he disagreed with me."

"Does it hurt?" Lily reached out in sympathy, but Gagne drew back.

"I'm okay, really."

Randolph slammed the phone down and their heads turned his way. "The good news is, the stage is nearly erected. The bad news—Chief Whitehorse had a heart attack, so he cannot deliver the blessing at the wilderness dedication." The mogul thrust himself from the chair and paced the floor. "How can we find a replacement on such short notice?" He turned to Lily and snapped his fingers. "Didn't you meet a Native American pastor the other day?"

"Charlie Waits," she said.

"See if you can get him to fill in."

Lily nodded obediently.

Randolph's eyes locked on his wife's midsection. "Have you gained weight?"

The blood drained from Lily's face.

Randolph's thin lips pressed together. "Maybe you'd better pick up the laps in that pool I built for you."

Gabor Gagne set his empty glass down hard on the table and stared at Randolph as if challenging him. "I think your wife is perfect."

"Of course," Randolph returned. "Yet perfection takes discipline."

Lily looked down, self-consciously brushed a hand across her abdomen and remained silent about her pregnancy.

CHAPTER 39

Begin to weave and God will give the thread.
—German proverb

Wyoming
Thursday, July 13

Reuben knelt beneath an overhang and offered the young woman water that he had cupped in the hollow of his hand. "You're lucky, Ma'am," he said as she drank. "An inch or two to the left and that branch may have done some serious damage."

"Please, call me Anna—Anna O'Neil." She shifted her weight and grimaced in pain from the nasty flesh wound on her side. Her fingers traced the makeshift bandage Reuben had ripped from his undershirt. "I thought I was going to die," she said quietly. "If you hadn't been there . . ."

Reuben studied her cautiously. A natural beauty with a wild tangle of short hair. "Why are you here?"

"I could ask you the same thing," Anna retorted.

She softened. "I'm sorry."

They fell silent as if they were both trying to assess each other.

"Why didn't you turn me in?" he asked.

Anna shrugged. "We're both in trouble. Guess I thought we could help each other. So, after I led Dudley Do-Right away from your lair, I doubled back to find you."

"I don't like the idea of having an injured woman along," Reuben said bluntly. "It's hard enough trying to survive on my own."

"Nobody's asking you to stay," Anna snapped. She rubbed her arm to stifle a shiver.

Reuben stood and offered her a hand. "We need to do something about your wet clothes. There's a sandbar on the other side of that boulder. It's warm. You can dry out and get some rest."

Anna stood carefully, cradled her ribs and shuffled to the boulder.

With his new charge out of the way, Reuben passed the afternoon fishing, using a Native American technique he had learned as a boy. Draped over a boulder near the river's edge, he dangled his hand in the water, letting it move like natural driftwood. The process required patience. An hour passed before he sensed movement beneath the cleft of the rock. A fish brushed past his skin. Slowly, patiently, Reuben's fingers stroked the fish's belly, lulling it. Finally, in a single motion, his hand closed around the tailfin and he tossed the fish ashore.

Anna was asleep when he returned to the sand bar. Reuben woke her and they ate.

"You mentioned trouble," he said between bites.

Anna sighed. "Somebody's trying to kill me."

"There's a lot of that going around." Reuben picked a bone from his fish. "So what's your story? Why would someone want you dead?"

"It's complicated," she said.

"I'll cancel my appointments."

The young woman chewed her lip. "The whole thing is crazy, but here goes. A long time ago, an old college friend of my father's, Jeffery Lyons, came up with a plan to defraud people."

"Nice friend," Reuben said.

"The general idea is this: Political groups are both energized and galvanized during times of imminent threat, such as war. To achieve the same effect during times of peace, enemies must be created."

"What kind of enemies?" Reuben tossed the fish bones in the river and knelt to wash his hands.

"Ecological disasters," Anna explained, picking at her food. "These could be fabricated or even staged. This, in turn, would generate public interest, money, and political capital."

"So that explains why we never hear any good news about the environment," Reuben said.

Anna bristled. "I'm a biologist. I've spent my whole life working in the field of ecology and a lot has been accomplished. There have been many environmental changes that are positive—new laws and regulations."

"That's my point. How come I don't read about these so-called accomplishments in the newspaper?"

Her eyes widened. "You know, someone else recently made the same observation."

"And do you agree?"

Anna's lips tightened defensively.

"Know what I think?" Reuben said. "Radical environmental organizations aren't interested in admitting success. If they did, they'd have to agree that the present system is working. That wouldn't be good for business." He combed his fingers through his scraggly beard. "It's just another example of man playing God."

"God has nothing to do with anything!" Anna retorted.

Reuben was surprised by her reaction. "How can anyone see this beautiful country and not believe in the God who made it?"

Anna twisted angrily and grimaced in pain.

Reuben lowered himself to the ground. He leaned back against the canyon wall, looked at the evening light upon the cliff, and pointed above their heads. "Do you see them?"

She leaned forward. "What?"

"Bats." Dozens of them sliced through the dark gray light.

"They remind me of the blind faith of a Christian," Anna said sarcastically. "Except for one thing—those creatures know there's a mosquito hatch to feed on. Christians don't know for sure there is a God."

Night began to fall. "You're wrong," Reuben said. "The evidence of God is everywhere. Maybe you're the one who's blind."

"I'm not deluded by religious myths," Anna huffed.

In spite of the static in the air, Reuben ventured on. "Are you sure about that? Let's talk about your religion."

"I don't have one."

"The way I see it, radical environmentalism is bound with the spiritual cords of many different religions: pantheism, animism, and Hinduism, to name a few. You can stir it all together and call it the New Age movement, but its still religion."

Anna wrinkled her brow. "What's your point?"

"I believe in a God who is big enough to create this planet, holy enough to give His word to man, and merciful enough to send His Son to die for my sins. You believe we're all just floating through the cosmos as tiny particles of a big impersonal organism. Admit it, Anna. You're carrying just as much religious baggage as anyone."

"That's ridiculous. I'm a scientist!" Anna shot to her feet and doubled over in pain.

Reuben offered a helping hand, but she knocked it away. "I didn't mean to offend you. Guess I'm just tired of

Christianity being vilified by a green theology that leaves man entirely out of the ecosystem."

"The environmental movement isn't perfect," Anna conceded. She settled back against the rock wall and issued a long sigh. "Maybe it is time to do things differently."

"Tell that to the people who were up here planting wolves."

"What?" Anna's eyes flashed. "Now you've gone too far. I'm involved in the reintroduction and all our wolves are accounted for. You've been filling your head with local anti-wolf propaganda. The wolf reintroduction plan is totally above board."

"Well, somebody threw in some ringers."

Anna's mouth dropped open. "I don't believe you."

"My father-in-law and I witnessed it personally."

"Why would anyone do that?"

"I've had a lot of time to think about that." Reuben tugged on his beard. "What would happen if there were confirmed gray wolf sightings before the planned reintroduction?"

Anna lifted a stick from the ground and tapped it on a boulder. "If the wolves migrated here naturally, they would be entitled to full protection under the Endangered Species Act."

"Would there be any way to prove whether these wolves were natural?" Reuben pressed.

"Probably not. If there were sightings, it would be assumed."

"That's what I thought." Reuben puffed air through his nostrils. "Three gray wolves were planted up on the mountain. I saw it with my own eyes. My father-in-law, Duke Bassett and I were on our way to set up camp when a helicopter landed in a meadow. They unloaded crates and . . ."

"Who would do such a thing?" Anna said.

Reuben studied the young woman's face, flushing with anger. "There were three men, two with uniforms I didn't recognize. One I've seen before—can't remember his name, but he hangs around with all the local eco-nuts. You probably know him. White hair, late fifties . . ."

"Addison Lee?"

"That's the name!"

"Whatever they were doing must have been legitimate," she said stiffly. "I've known Addison for years and he's always done things properly."

"Yeah?" Reuben picked up a rock and lobbed it toward the river. "That explains why he shot my father-in-law in the back."

Anna gasped. "No!"

"He was leaning out the window of the helicopter with a rifle in his hand. Would have got me too, but I ran for a thicket."

"Why didn't you go back to town and tell the sheriff?" she challenged.

"Thought I saw the pilot and the third guy were wearing uniforms. I didn't know who to trust. In fact, I'm not even sure if I should trust you." Reuben turned inward as his thoughts replayed that that fateful day.

"It seems incredible . . ." Anna's voice trailed off.

Reuben picked up a piece of driftwood and ran his finger over its smooth surface. "The Addison Lees of this world think they've got it all figured out—believe they're better than people like me. I know plenty of folks who make their living from this land and I have yet to meet one who doesn't go out of his way to protect the resources. There's no doubt about it. We need to conserve. But, as far as I can tell, the yahoos you hang around with don't seem to be interested in finding solutions."

Wordless minutes passed as the rapids churned nearby. Finally Anna spoke. "We've got to expose the lie—lay the whole thing wide open." Her eyes locked onto Reuben's. "And I think I know just how to do it."

In the cradle of the canyon, the air began to chill. "I'm listening," he said.

CHAPTER 40

Traditus non victus—Betrayed, not conquered.
Latin proverb

Wyoming
Thursday, July 13

From her bedroom window, Lily saw the luxury touring bus wind up the road toward the mansion. Delilah Harris was arriving with all the fanfare Randolph had warned her to expect. The bus, with Delilah's diamond logo on the side, rolled past the front door and idled to a stop just out of view.

Lily drew back and closed her eyes, letting her imagination take her downstairs. She envisioned Randolph, smooth and calm among the flurry of excitement. He would kiss Delilah's cheek and offer refreshments. Lily wondered if the actress was nervous, for if Randolph chose to do so, he had the power to squash Delilah's career.

The intercom buzzed. "Mrs. Harrington, your

husband requests your presence."

Lily glanced in the mirror at her western riding skirt and simple white blouse. It was an improvement from the frilly outfits that Randolph wanted her to wear. Lily smoothed her shiny hair, applied some lip gloss, and hurried downstairs to greet their guest.

Delilah Harris was larger than life, with big hair, big jewelry, and a full figure; she filled the room with her presence. "You must be Lily!" She floated across the room with arms wide open and swallowed her hostess in clouds of expensive perfume. "I've heard delicious things about you, love," Delilah gushed. "But I must say, they haven't done you justice." The starlet held Lily captive, brushing her gaze across her like a paintbrush. "You are simply stunning. No, that is too light a word. Breathtaking!" Delilah winked at Randolph. "You have impeccable taste, darling."

He seemed pleased, even energized by Delilah's presence.

Lily extricated herself with an awkward "Thank you." She tried to think of something else to say, but her mind went blank.

Fortunately, their other house guest stepped forward. Like a knight rescuing her from the dragon's lair, Gabor Gagne took over, chatting easily with the actress. "Good weather is expected for the dedication. And from what I hear, there will be quite a turnout."

Lily received a glass of ginger ale from one of the

maids and casually observed her husband. His eyes narrowed and his mouth pinched into a scowl. He seemed jealous of the attention the actress was giving Gabor.

"An enormous amount of planning has gone into this event," Randolph interjected. He moved stiffly across the room and handed Delilah a glass of sherry. "I presume this is still your favorite drink?"

"You know me too well." She took a sip and wiped her lip with a long acrylic nail.

The evening wore on, with Delilah hanging on Randolph's words like a smitten schoolgirl.

After dinner, Lily watched her husband whisper in the actress's ear. Delilah threw her head back in laughter and playfully touched Randolph's cheek.

"They're just old friends," Gabor said. He seemed to sense Lily's distress. "They've known each other for years."

Lily forced a smile and took a sip from her glass. "I wish I could be as confident as she is."

Gabor laughed and swirled the wine in his crystal goblet. "I find you real and refreshing."

Lily felt buoyed by the compliment. Despite her husband's preoccupation with Delilah Harris, she managed to endure the evening with a measure of grace.

At 11:00 PM, Gabor excused himself and Lily approached her husband.

"You look tired, Wildflower," he said. "Run along to bed. I'll be up shortly."

"Yes," Delilah intoned, "I need my beauty rest, too." The actress sauntered over to the bar. "But first, a little nightcap."

Lily excused herself and went upstairs. In bed she lay awake, feeling frightened. Uninvited thoughts rolled through her mind, thoughts too scary for words. Was her world crumbling? Would it be so bad if it all fell apart?

Lily summoned courage and rose from her bed. With stealth, she padded softly down the stairs. Randolph and Delilah were in the den—she could hear them. Standing on the hard tile floor, Lily felt a chill wash over her. With a shaky hand, she approached the door. It was ajar. She peeked inside.

There they were—her husband entangled in the arms of another woman.

—m—

Wyoming
Thursday, July 13

Lily drove from the mountain amidst a slurry of tears, wondering where she could run to. Charlie came to mind.

When she pulled up to his mobile home, she saw a television light flickering through the window. *Good,* she thought, wiping tear-soaked hair from her face. He was still up.

She knocked, waited, then knocked again. Her

knees shook in the mountain air and she realized for the first time that she had fled barefoot. A minute passed. Lily knocked louder and saw movement through the door's frosted glass window.

A young man answered, leaning on crutches. He looked dark and tattered. Lily stepped back. "Is . . . Is Charlie here?"

"Yeah." With an indifferent cock of his head, he motioned Lily inside.

"I didn't know anyone else lived here. I mean . . . I hope I'm not disturbing you."

He smirked as though he found humor in her self-conscious fumbling. "I'll get Charlie."

Lily watched him maneuver his crutches down the trailer's narrow corridor.

A few moments later, the pastor appeared, cinching the belt on his robe and shuffling toward her in sheepskin slippers.

"I know it's late," Lily said, "but I didn't know where else to go."

"You're always welcome." The pastor rubbed sleep from his eyes and invited Lily to sit on his old plaid couch.

The younger man switched off the television with the end of his crutch.

"This is Peter, my . . ." The young man shot Charlie a warning look. "My house guest."

"Nice to meet you," Lily said.

"I'm going to bed." Peter hobbled down the hall.

She heard a door close hard and wondered if coming here was a mistake. Loneliness descended upon Lily like a fog.

"Do you drink coffee?" Charlie asked from the kitchen.

"Tea," she called.

He emerged with a bag of Oreo cookies. "I put the kettle on." The pastor settled on the couch beside Lily. In a fatherly gesture, he reached for her hand. "What's troubling you?"

"I've left my husband." She suppressed the urge to cry. "I don't know what's real anymore. I used to believe in love, but now . . ."

Down the hallway, Lily noticed the bedroom door ajar and realized Peter was probably listening. It didn't matter—nothing mattered.

"There is always hope," Charlie said.

"You really believe that." It was more a statement than a question. "How?"

Charlie looked across the room and fixed his eyes on a ceramic cross that hung on the wall.

The teakettle whistled and Charlie hurried into the kitchen. He returned with two steaming mugs and set them on the coffee table next to the cookies.

Lily lowered her head. "Do you think God could give me hope too?"

"He's been waiting for you to ask."

Charlie offered his hand, and in the modest trailer house, Lily prayed what the pastor called "the sinner's prayer."

"You're one of God's kids now." Charlie's eyebrows rose and he appeared to be studying Lily. "You may not realize it just yet, but you've just received salvation—a gift more precious than gold."

Something stirred in Lily's heart—it felt good.

After sipping their tea and munching on Oreos, Charlie asked, "Want to talk about your husband?"

"I never want to see him again," she said resolutely. "He'll never change."

"Maybe not. But you have."

Lily looked down at her hands. She knew the pastor was right and her sense of indignation weakened. "Randolph won't even know I'm gone. And tomorrow he'll be busy with the wilderness dedication."

"That's right!" Charlie said. "I'm giving the invocation. Why don't we go together and see what tomorrow brings?" The pastor pushed up from the couch and checked the Big Ben clock on the table. It was 1:00 AM. "I'll bring you some blankets and a pillow. It's always better to deal with things after a good night's rest."

"I'm not sure I can fall asleep."

He grinned and handed her a Bible. "I know a great book."

"Thanks, Pastor Charlie," Lily said with a grateful heart. "Thanks for everything."

CHAPTER 41

Perfer et obdura; multo graviora tulisti—
endure and persist;
this pain will turn to your good by and by.
Latin-Ovid

Wyoming
Friday, July 14

Anna's wound throbbed and she felt chilled to the bone, but she had pushed on through the night without complaint. She and Reuben had been moving in the dark for what seemed like an eternity. She figured they had maybe three hours until sunrise. The biggest danger now was not the men who combed the mountainside, but the threat of hypothermia. Reuben had insisted they soak their clothing in the cold stream to avoid detection by infrared scopes.

Anna's teeth chattered as they trudged down a rugged game trail. She stumbled over a tree root, but clambered back to her weary feet. In the faint light, she could just make out the rugged path, surprised by how good her night vision was.

Reuben waited silently for his unlikely partner as she slid down a rocky knob. "Cold?" he asked.

"Don't worry about me," she said stubbornly. "I'll warm up down in the lowlands." Anna ignored her mounting hunger and muscle fatigue and pressed on. The descent was quicker than she had expected and soon they made it to the foothills. From there, they moved with stealth to an adjacent field.

"Let's rest here for a few minutes." Reuben dropped into a dry ditch that ran between rows of young barley plants. Settling into its hollow, he motioned for Anna to join him. "This will give us cover for a while, but we'll have to crawl. After that, we'll need to improvise."

Anna looked toward the dusky sky. "I hope we can get to the meadow before people arrive."

"We'll make it." Reuben said. "Don't have a choice."

With the resolve of a fighter, Anna crawled onward. "I haven't prepared a speech for the wilderness dedication," she said dryly.

"You'll think of something."

The Pristine Valley came into view as the morning sun began to glow just over the horizon. They stopped at the river so Reuben could assess the situation. Intermittent stands of aspens offered breaks in the flat bottom, except at the point where the river meandered through the meadow. There, the waters spread wide and shallow, with nothing but grass and wildflowers at its bank. "No cover," Rueben mumbled. "It's not going to be easy."

Anna's attentions were elsewhere. She gazed past the meadow to a massive stage—its wooden platform studded with microphones. "That's where the wilderness dedication will take place."

"You sure they're not having a Rolling Stones concert here?" Reuben said with a cynical smirk. His tone turned serious. "Anyway, we've got a problem that needs solving."

Anna looked back toward the mountain. "If the trackers picked up our trail, don't you think they'd be on us by now?"

"Probably," Reuben said, "but we can't take chances. We have to make it across that low point without being seen and that's a lot of flat ground."

Anna cupped her hands over her eyes. In the field, a herd of horses grazed in the dawning light. A swaybacked mare ambled toward the river. "Maybe the hand of divine providence is with us after all," Anna said hopefully. The horse whinnied slightly and clomped across the rocky bottom for a drink of frigid water.

Reuben crept up to the animal. Before she could lift her head from the river, he fastened his belt around her neck. "I'll walk behind her front shoulder; you crouch behind her back. Try to match the movements of her legs." The old mare seemed grateful for the company as she escorted them across the meadow.

By the time the sun's rays had fanned across the valley, the fugitives were safely hidden beneath the stage—the safest place from prying eyes. The mare grazed nearby for a while, then wandered off.

"When the stage crew arrives, they'll be all over this stage," he pointed to some wires dangling near-by. "There's a thick stand of Willows out back. We'll hide there until all the bugs are worked out of the sound system." Reuben said "We can slip back here later."

"Okay." Anna contemplated the mud under her fingernails. "What if my plan to expose the whole eco scam doesn't work?" she said.

Reuben put his hands behind his head and settled back in the shadows. "Do you have any other choice?"

Anna knew the truth must be told. Below the stage's platform, she crouched low among the trampled meadow grass. From there, she peeked through the stage's canvas skirting. Judging from the elaborate media platforms outside—the wilderness dedication was going to be a big event. Anna tried to imagine Randolph Harrington's reaction to her new perspective. He wouldn't be happy, that's for sure. Anna's heart fluttered with anxiety as she realized what was at stake—her career— even her reputation.

Anna spread a piece of canvas skirting, tucked it in the trusses, and settled in a patch of sunlight that spilled beneath the stage. The cloudless Wyoming sky seemed to go on forever. Somewhere beneath this eternal blue canopy, a backpack was floating down the river with The Canaan Creed CD. She wondered how she could pull this thing off without proof. Insecurity rolled over Anna.

The faint hum of a motor met her ear. A vehicle was grinding slowly up the dirt road, and Anna caught a glint of chrome through the trees. She woke Reuben from his nap. "Someone's coming."

He was at her side in a flash. "Let's move." He motioned for Anna to follow. Quickly, they slid under the skirting and hurried to the tangle of willows.

Soon the pristine meadow was bustling with activity. Anna watched nearly a hundred crewmembers trudge about, lugging supplies and hammering nails. Randolph Harrington had spared no expense to create the perfect blend of Hollywood and nature. By noon, the PA system was up and running.

Anna and Reuben waited until the crew broke for lunch before returning to their hiding place beneath the stage. "They must expect a sold-out crowd," he said, noting the crew setting up rows of chairs.

A caravan of vehicles snaked up the road. The media had arrived. The crews spilled from their vans, barking directives. A manic flurry of arms, legs, and microphones ensued.

Reuben cocked his head and peered between the flaps. "You hear that? A chopper."

"Move over." Anna nudged Reuben aside just in

time to see the helicopter swoop over the skyline. It hovered to a landing on the flat meadow. As the blades wound down, the stage crew gathered to welcome the passengers.

From the dark shadows beneath the stage, Anna and Reuben watched two men and a woman emerge from the helicopter.

"The man with dark hair is Randolph Harrington," Anna explained. "The other one is Gabor Gagne, founder of the Endangered Earth Alliance. And the woman . . ."

"Delilah Harris," Reuben interrupted. "This Harrington guy has thrown together a nice carnival. I can't wait 'till they set up the cotton candy stand."

Anna spotted Gabor Gagne, who was observing the whole affair from the sidelines with a look of disgust. Her eyes shifted to Randolph who strode around giving last-minute orders. A few yards away from him, the starlet threw out her arms, theatrically exclaimed the virtues of fresh air, and fluttered among the crew, drawing attention.

Anna felt depression settle over her. *How had it come to this?*

CHAPTER 42

I have seen all the works that are done under the sun;
and indeed, all is vanity and grasping for the wind.
Ecclesiastes 1:14

Wyoming
Friday, July 14

Wedged between Charlie and Peter in the pastor's old truck, Lily bounced up the dirt road, feeling like a kid on a trampoline.

"Pristine Meadows is just over the rise," Charlie said. "One of the prettiest spots on earth if you ask me."

Lily didn't respond. Her thoughts were as deep as the ruts in the rustic mountain road. Repeatedly her mind replayed her husband's betrayal. How could she forgive him?

The truck turned sharply up a switchback. Charlie slowed down and rocked over a series of rocks. "Peter, that photo of yours was taken up here at Pristine Meadows. I gave your mother the camera on our anniversary."

The young man appeared indifferent, but Lily sensed his interest. "Are you two related?"

"Hardly," Peter said sharply.

Lily's intuition warned her not to pry. Besides, she had her own problems. A fresh surge of emotion swelled in her heart and threatened to break anew. She bit her lip and swallowed the pain.

From behind, an SUV honked impatiently. "Do you suppose they want me to pull over?" Charlie said with a wink. The road was barely big enough for one car. To the right was a steep side hill and to the left a treacherous cliff. "If they're in a hurry they can pass me."

The old pickup topped the pass and rounded a small knob before rolling toward the meadow. New wild wheat waved among tender sprouts of grass. The SUV steered off the road and accelerated around Charlie, showering his old truck with flower-laden dirt clods.

"Must be a nature lover," the old man chuckled.

On the far end of the meadow, several dozen cars were parked.

Charlie pulled into the lot and hopped from the truck. "What did I tell you?" He threw his arms out with enthusiasm. "With these jagged peaks all around, it looks like we're standing in the center of a majestic crown!"

Lily spotted her husband on the stage: Randolph Harrington, king of the mountain. He was engaged in animated conversation with Gabor Gagne and one of

Wyoming's senators. Lily's heart skipped a beat.

"Would you like me to come with you?" Charlie asked.

Lily declined the offer. She needed to do this herself.

As she neared the stage, Randolph looked up, hastily excused himself, and hurried down the steps. "Where have you been?" he asked, grabbing his wife's arm.

"I saw what happened last night." Lily twisted her arm from his grasp. "I needed to sort things out."

"Whatever you believe took place last night is irrelevant. No one ever walks out on Randolph Harrington." His words were controlled but threatening. "Do I make myself clear?"

Lily blinked, but said nothing.

Her husband's gaze shifted. "I see you brought your Native American friend like I asked." Randolph looked over her head and snapped his fingers at a man wearing a black ball cap "Bring me a copy of the invocation."

The man riffled through a strong box near the edge of the stage, produced a paper, and hurried it down the stairs to his boss. Randolph looked the page over and handed it to Lily. "Great Native American prayer," he said, "Give this to your pastor friend."

"Is that all you have to say to me?" Lily said.

"We will discuss our personal issues later." Then

he added, "You look as though you slept in your clothing. Do yourself a favor, Wildflower, and avoid the cameras."

As Lily watched her husband walk away, an odd feeling of peace held her. She had not crumbled in his shadow.

More people arrived. The crowd thickened and a cloud of fine dust hung in the air from the heavy foot traffic. At the media center, Delilah Harris drew crowds of eager fans and churned out autographs with relish. Lily watched the whole event with a strange detachment.

She located Charlie and gave him the papers as Randolph had instructed.

When he finished reading, Charlie scratched his head and stared up at the mountain.

"What's wrong?" she asked.

"This is a Native American prayer about Mother Earth and her virtues."

Peter leaned over Charlie's shoulder and read aloud. "Beloved Mother Earth, benevolent and kind, we are all your children. Hear us now as we serve and honor you, our sustainer. Accept this dedication as a worshipful offering." The young man shrugged. "It's not so bad."

Charlie shook his head. "I can't read this."

"Why not?" Peter demanded. He stabbed at a grasshopper with his crutch and watched it fly away.

"I cannot pray to Mother Earth."

"So you would embarrass yourself in front of all these people for this so-called God of yours?"

"Yes." Charlie leaned against an old cottonwood tree. "I'd rather look like a fool than to speak words I don't believe."

Peter swung his crutch toward the mountain. "Don't you care about the earth?"

Charlie turned his face upward. "Not a day goes by that I don't thank God for his beautiful creation."

"So, what's the problem?" The young man's words were caustic, but Charlie remained steadfast.

"The Bible says that the land suffers decay when the people who inhabit it refuse to worship the Creator."

"You mean like a curse?" Peter asked.

Charlie thought for a moment. "I guess you could put it that way. More like the blessing of the Lord taken away. Still, the result is the same. The very people who think they're saving the earth may actually be causing its destruction."

Lily considered her husband in light of Charlie's words and felt a wave of pity for the man who thought of himself as a savior of the world. Randolph had vowed to save the earth, just as he had vowed to love, honor, and cherish his wife.

CHAPTER 43

If folly were grief, every house would weep.
George Herbert

Wyoming
Friday, July 14

Grace sprinkled flour on the biscuit dough and kneaded it with gusto, but the activity could not ease her worried mind. Her husband had not come to bed last night. She'd found him sitting in the dark kitchen, staring blankly into space. Milo ignored her coaxing, and by 2:00 AM, Grace gave up and returned to bed. She woke in a sweat, gripped by a fear she had never known.

Milo was still in the kitchen. She kissed his cheek. Grace made coffee and small talk. Without a word, her husband shoved away from the table and trudged down into the storage room. Deadness seemed to permeate the air.

Now, in the comfort and familiarity of the café, Grace fought the urge to weep. The breakfast crowd would

be bearing down soon. Maybe she should just close up—
take the day off. But someone needed to hold things
together. Grace wiped her hands on her apron, moved to
the wall phone and called her daughter-in-law.

"Honey, Milo's not feeling well today," she said.

"I'll come right over. I hope it isn't the flu. The
usual flu season is over, but you never know."

By the time the breakfast crowd began to trickle in,
the Fischer Creek Café was bursting with the aroma of
Grace's fresh-baked biscuits and cinnamon rolls. With
pencil and order pad in hand, Jody worked the tables,
filling the customers' ears with chatter and their mugs with
coffee.

Grace busied herself at the grill, rolling sizzling
sausages and frying eggs. She pulled a tray of steaming
rolls from the oven and placed them on the baker's rack.
Grace moved to the back door and her thoughts drifted to
down the thirty-two stone steps that led to the cabin she
shared with her husband. Her unease grew. "Jody," she
called, "I'm going down to check on Milo."

Grace removed her apron, hung it on the peg by
the kitchen door, and walked down to the cabin. All was
quiet inside. She stepped across the creaky wooden floor,
calling her husband's name. No answer. The door to
Milo's workroom stood ajar. "Honey?" She pushed it
open, but her husband was not there. Spread haphazardly
across his rustic workbench was a newspaper. An article
had been torn from its pages. Beside it was an empty box

of rifle shells.

Grace whirled around to check Milo's gun cabinet. His rifle was missing!

She hurried back to the café, wheezing for air and clutching her pounding chest.

Jody shot over to her mother-in-law's side. "Grace, are you sick? I hope you aren't catching what Milo has. Can I get you a glass of water?"

Grace shook her head and reached for a newspaper on the counter. She unfolded it and located the article Milo had clipped. "Pristine Valley Wilderness Dedication Draws Hollywood's Eco Elite."

"Oh, no," Grace whispered. "Please, no."

—⁓—

Wyoming
Friday, July 14

Investigator Jay Corpizio finished reading the article on the wilderness dedication. He folded the paper and looked across the bench seat of the suburban. Special Agent Iverson turned the wheel and headed up the mountain road. "So you think Anna O'Neil will show up at this thing?"

"I have no idea." The agent looked in the rearview mirror. "What do you think, Chaz?"

"I'm betting she'll show," his partner said. "She's listed as one of the speakers, so it's worth checking out."

"Let me see if I have this straight," Corpizio said. "You believe there's a network of moles working within our government and they're trying to further some kind of rogue environmental agenda?"

"We've been conducting an internal investigation," Agent Iverson explained. "The ecology angle may just be a front. We believe it's really about political and financial power."

Corpizio tossed the newspaper to the side. "You have evidence?"

"We could make a dozen arrests today, but that might drive Jeffery Lyons further underground." The car rolled over a cattle guard and turned up the mountain road.

"And Malcolm O'Neil was about to blow Lyons's cover?"

"This guy is dangerous," Chaz said. "He'll do anything to protect his secret."

CHAPTER 44

*The whole art of war consists in
getting at what is on the other side of the hill.*

Aurthur Wellesley—1st Duke of Wellington

Wyoming
Friday, July 14

The New Age rock band burst into song, the primal beat of its drums resonating beneath the stage. Anna looked at Reuben. "This is it."

He raised his eyebrows. "Ready?"

"That's a rhetorical question, right?" Anna crawled to the back and carefully maneuvered around a tangle of speaker wires. She lifted the canvas flap, her heart keeping time with the drums. "How do I look? Never mind, I don't really want to know."

Reuben didn't say a word.

Anna grinned. "That bad, huh?" Behind the stage, she quickly fluffed her dusty hair and rubbed smudges from her face. With shoulders squared, Anna walked to the rows of VIP chairs to look for a seat facing center-stage.

The rock band's lead singer shrieked, "Gaia, Gaia, goddess of the earth, shine on your children." Among the enthusiastic crowd, Anna slipped discreetly into a seat, unnoticed except by Addison Lee, who acknowledged her with a wave.

When the song ended, Randolph Harrington took the microphone. "Ladies and gentlemen, I am greatly encouraged that so many of you have come to celebrate with us here today." The mogul's gaze fanned across the crowd of five hundred plus. "I'm especially pleased to see so many young people, the future torchbearers of deep ecology. Let us give our youth a round of applause."

After a rousing response, Randolph introduced Pastor Charlie Waits. "Please join with this Native American holy man as he pays tribute to this spectacular planet . . . my church," he added reverently.

Anna recognized the friendly-faced pastor as a local man, though she had never spoken with him.

"Thank you." Charlie cleared his throat. "But if any holiness is found in me, it is only to the credit of my Lord and Savior, Jesus Christ." He looked at the audience. "I was asked to read a prayer today, but I am led to pray in a different way." Pastor Waits closed his soft brown eyes and lowered his head. "Lord," he began, "may this ceremony be dedicated entirely to You. May we honor and respectfully acknowledge You as the maker of all creation."

Curious whispers rippled through the crowd as Randolph hastily retrieved the microphone. "Well, that was certainly unexpected, but nice." Harrington stood stiffly as Charlie left the platform. His eyes locked on Anna, who was nestled among the elite. "I see the prestigious Gaia award winner has decided to join us after all." Randolph flashed a white smile. "It looks as though our Anna' O'Neil has been communing with nature." The crowd looked her way.

"We will hear from our young biologist shortly, but first, I would like to introduce a gentleman who has sacrificed all for this wonderful living planet. This man's distinguished credits include saving the blue dolphin from extinction by successfully lobbying for government regulation of the tuna fishing industry's practices. He has courageously stared down the cold barrel of progress to protect the South American rain forests. For years, this man has warned industrialized nations about pollution and the evils of genetically engineered food. However, his most urgent cry in the wilderness concerns the imminent threat of global warming. Please give a warm welcome to the founder of the Endangered Earth Alliance, Gabor Gagne."

The audience thundered with applause as Gabor walked on stage. He held the microphone to his mouth. "Thank you." He seemed ill at ease on stage—not surprising for a man once known as a recluse. "I was just in the neighborhood and thought I'd drop by for a visit."

The people laughed, the tension broke, and Gabor seemed to relax.

His words touched a cord in Anna. He had said the same thing the other day when he called her at home—not so unusual, but there was something else, something she couldn't put her finger on.

"I'm happy to be here with you good people," Gagne said. "But the message I bring is a somber one. As Randolph said, the threat of global warming is imminent. This man-made monster is on the march: melting glaciers, rising sea levels, floods, droughts, hurricanes, and even insect proliferation can all be attributed to the rising temperatures caused by global warming. Up to 25 percent of the world's species are on the brink of destruction."

A profound silence fell among the audience and Gabor gave his words time to settle. "Will you join with me in saving our dying planet?"

The people echoed their allegiance.

Gabor's speech continued, but Anna was indifferent to his words. Something didn't fit.

Suddenly, she heard her name. "Please welcome our own Anna O'Neil." She snapped from her haze to see Randolph Harrington beckoning her to the podium.

There was no turning back. Anna felt herself inching toward the edge of a precipice. She took her place beside Randolph amidst an enthusiastic chorus of applause and whistles.

The mogul's flatteries were lost on Anna as she

stood in the limelight. "Champion of our cause," she heard him say. "Selfless harbinger of change . . ."

I can't do this, she thought with sudden panic. Her knees shook and she wondered if her nervousness showed.

"And now, without further ado . . ." Randolph handed Anna the microphone and stepped back. The applause dwindled to silence.

She looked at the faces of those who had been friends and colleagues. Her head began to spin. "Change," she began. "That's what I want to talk about." The crowd settled at attention. "We've heard a lot about threats like global warming. But I want to address another immediate threat." Anna paused to gather courage. "There are enemies among us. They walk like stewards, they talk like ecologists, but their motive is greed and lust for power." Anna licked her lips. "These imposters have grown among us like an invasive, noxious weed, scattering seeds of false data and fear. It's time to uproot them."

A murmur rippled through the crowd, but Anna pressed on, deliberately refusing to look at Randolph. "The idea for this grand-scale deception was birthed many years ago by a man named Jeffery Lyons and it is outlined in a document called The Canaan Creed."

Randolph Harrington hurried to Anna's side. "Very interesting, Ms. O'Neil, but I must remind you that we are here to talk about the Pristine Wilderness Dedication." His fingers coiled around the microphone, but Anna grasped it firmly.

"Tree spiking. Illegal introduction of wolves. Junk science. Fear mongering. Possibly even murder. These are some of the things the proponents of this plan are capable of."

The crowd grew restless. Someone heckled Anna, yet she refused to back down. "Innocent lives are being destroyed. It is time to take back what we have built on sound principles of ecology. In the spirit of cooperation, we need to reach across the divide of mistrust."

Randolph summoned a couple of stagehands.

"We will either change or go down with this ship!" Anna relinquished the microphone to Randolph and allowed the stagehands to escort her peacefully from the stage.

From the platform, Randolph Harrington offered a flurry of apologetic words. "Our poor Anna has been under a tremendous strain lately. You may have heard. Her father died recently. She's been confused."

Anna felt the heat of hostile eyes as she was ushered to her seat. *My career is over,* she thought.

Soon after she sat, a warm hand touched her shoulder. Anna turned to see Gabor Gagne kneeling on the ground beside her.

"You're right," he whispered. "There is always room for change."

"You believe me?" Anna felt a rush of relief.

He leaned close and spoke softly. "Maybe I can help. Do you have proof of these allegations?"

Anna felt his hot breath on her cheek as she looked into his eyes. "You were just in the neighborhood?" she muttered as the pieces fell into place.

"Excuse me?"

"You said it when you called my house and then again when you were on stage," Anna said. "And you said the same thing on my father's answering machine." She stood and backed away. "It was you!"

"What are you saying?" Gabor looked confused.

"Did you call my father to reminisce about your college days?"

Gabor's eyes narrowed

"You are Jeffery Lyons."

Gabor grabbed Anna's arm. "Let's go somewhere quiet where we can discuss this."

She felt the barrel of a gun against her ribs.

"Don't make a scene." His face looked calm and friendly, but his voice was low and threatening. Gabor walked Anna around the stage and forced her over to the thick stand of willows.

"Is this how you discussed things with Malcolm?"

Gagne's lips jerked into an odd smile. "With the exception of a few tiny loose ends, I think I've covered my tracks well. My only mistake was accepting the Man of the Year title for *Time* magazine. Your father recognized me."

"What about William Vonsetter?"

Lyons sneered. "He was no threat. Everyone saw

him as a delusional scientist. But Malcolm and you, I'm sorry to say, are another story."

His arms wrapped around Anna's neck. "You should have taken my job offer. I could have made you a rich woman."

Anna struggled as he squeezed. "You won't get away with this," she gasped. "You were seen with me."

"Ah, but you were alive when I left you. Distraught, but alive. I will say I was trying to comfort you after you single-handedly destroyed your career." He increased the pressure. "They will find you here, hanging from your belt. I can see the headlines now: 'Biologist Anna O'Neil Takes Her Own Life.'"

Stars danced in Anna's head. She felt faint.

With a sudden jolt, Jeffery Lyons pitched forward. Anna tumbled to her knees.

Reuben stooped beside her, holding a good-sized rock in his hand. "Are you okay?"

She coughed and gasped for air. "I think so."

"I heard the whole thing." He offered her a hand.

Anna climbed to her feet and rubbed her neck. "What took you so long?"

CHAPTER 45

Be not deceived; God is not mocked;
for whatever a man sows, that he will also reap.
Galatians 6:7

Wyoming
Friday, July 14

Lily studied her husband's face. To the general public, Randolph appeared unruffled by the strange turn of events, but his plastic smile and rigid mannerisms gave him away. The reigns of control had slipped from his iron-fisted grip and he had been publicly embarrassed. Lily shuddered, and she felt a rush of pity for Anna O'Neil.

Things were winding down as Randolph prepared to introduce one of Wyoming's senators. After that, there would be photo ops and interviews with the stable of reporters.

A shot rang out! The crack of its report echoed from the mountain's rock face, leaving stunned silence in its wake. Confused conversation bubbled from the rows of folding chairs and heads turned. Someone screamed and pointed toward the stage.

Lily rose from her seat in horror. She watched her husband grip his chest and stagger forward. "Randolph!" she screamed as he fell to his knees.

Randolph Harrington drew his hand away from his chest and stared at blood-covered fingers. He looked up. "I've been shot."

Pandemonium broke out as the senator and the other VIPs were whisked off the stage. Another shot cracked through the valley, spinning the crowd into a whirlwind of confusion.

People exited the stage in panic. Against the flow, Lily pushed her way up the stairs to the platform. When she reached Randolph, his eyes fluttered weakly and he reached for his wife.

Lily dropped to the floor and took his hand. "You'll be okay."

Her husband opened his mouth and a ribbon of blood trickled from the corner of his lips.

"Don't talk. Save your strength." Lily squeezed Randolph's fingers and felt his grip relax. "Somebody help!" she yelled as she watched a growing pool of blood form under his limp body.

—m—

Wyoming
Friday, July 14

"Look!" Peter pointed toward the parking lot, where a bald-headed man emerged from behind a car with a rifle at his shoulder.

"That's Milo Fischer!" Charlie stood abruptly, knocking over his chair. Before Peter could react, his father set out across the meadow. Peter stood—not knowing what else to do.

"Milo," Charlie said, holding out his hand, "give me the gun?"

The armed man lowered the rifle and scowled. "Don't come any closer, Pastor. I've got no problem with you. It's those high rollers and bleeding-heart tree huggers who want to tell us how to live."

"We can work things out," Charlie reasoned.

"Yeah? Tell that to my grandson, Cordell. Tell that to Dillon, who can't earn a decent living because of the regulations they shove down our throats!"

"You've made your point." Charlie took another step closer. "Just give me the gun and we'll talk about it."

Milo's finger twitched on the trigger as he raised the rifle to his shoulder. "I'll shoot you if I have to."

Charlie shook his head and cautiously moved forward. "You wouldn't do that."

"Get out of my way!" Milo screamed.

Peter watched Charlie close the gap. He had never

seen such courage—his father, risking his own life for others.

"I warned you." Milo convulsed with rage and stared down the barrel.

Peter closed his eyes. The sound of another gunshot brought down an avalanche of regrets. He never even gave his father a chance.

But when Peter looked again, it was Milo, not Charlie, who lay dying on the ground.

—◊◊◊—

Wyoming
Friday, July 14

"I saw the whole thing," Corpizio assured Agent Iverson, slapping a sympathetic hand on his shoulder. "You had to shoot. The man was clearly a threat."

The FBI man slipped his gun back into the holster. "I'll get the sheriff and call for a medevac team." He turned to his partner. "Chaz, go check the shooter."

Corpizio had seen the placement of the bullet; he knew the shot was fatal. "I'll patrol the grounds."

Near the epicenter of the dedication ceremony, word of the gunman's death had spread like lightning. A wide gamut of emotions manifested among the traumatized crowd. Women sobbed, men blustered, some people just stood around pale and idle, and still others tried to calm the crowds.

"Corpizio?"

He turned to see Anna O'Neil, looking as if she had just come home from a safari.

"What are you doing here?" she asked. "Never mind," Anna grabbed the investigator's elbow. "Do you know first aid?" Without waiting for an answer, she tugged him up the stage stairs and pointed. Near the microphones lay a man, unmoving. Beside him, a young woman wept.

Corpizio felt for a pulse and shook his head. "I'm afraid he's gone."

"No," the young woman cried. "This is Randolph Harrington. He can't die!"

Anna touched the woman's shoulder. "I'm sorry, Lily."

Anna and Corpizio led Lily from the stage and summoned some of the stagehands to help.

Corpizio tapped Anna on the shoulder. "We need to talk."

Another agent stepped forward. "We believe a man named Jeffery Lyons is responsible for your father's death. He's living under an assumed name."

Anna motioned to Corpizio. "Come with me." The lawmen followed as she marched to a stand of trees and pointed to the base of a cottonwood. There a man lay, bound and gagged.

"Gentlemen," Anna announced. "I'd like to introduce you to Gabor Gagne, also know as Jeffery Lyons."

—ɯ—

Wyoming
Friday, July 14

Reuben held his father as the last thread of life escaped from Milo's wounded body. "Why?" he lamented.

The local sheriff lifted a handful of dirt and watched it trickle through his fingers. "We might never know what was going through Milo's mind when he pointed that rifle at these folks," Sheriff Hodge said. "Your dad was under tremendous stress. A lot happened while you were away."

Reuben listened to the tale of sabotage: gas tampering, arson, nails on a mountain road, and finally the malicious act of tree spiking that nearly took the life of his own son.

His fist curled in anger. "It feels like a war," Reuben said.

Hodge brushed dirt from his hands. He pushed up the brim of his hat. "Was it like that up on the mountain?" he asked carefully. "Like Vietnam?"

Reuben looked wearily at the sheriff. "I'm not shell-shocked, if that's what you mean. And I wasn't having a flashback."

"Why don't you start from the beginning, son?" Sheriff Hodge coaxed.

Reuben told him everything—about the wolves, Duke's death, and the attempts on his life.

"That's an incredible story," the sheriff said. "But a lot of strange things have been going on around here. Let's sort it all out back at the station." The sheriff pulled a pair of handcuffs from his jacket. He paused and looked earnestly at his prisoner. "Maybe it is a like a war—a war of ideologies."

Reuben offered his hands to the restraints. *It's out of my control*, he thought with a relief for the truth was on his side.

EPILOGUE

Wyoming;
Late June—nearly one year later

Anna O'Neil leaned against the jeep, still warm from the drive to her favorite spot up on Table Rock. Beneath a clear blue sky, the Pristine Valley spread from east to west like a panorama. It had been a long, difficult year. Old friends had turned away—some she never really knew, like Addison Lee, who had confessed to arson, gas tampering, malicious wounding, and finally the murder of Duke Bassett.

The community was healing, moving on. Yet Anna had been unable to find closure, until the phone call.

In the early morning hours, Corpizio called. "The jury finally reached a verdict. They found Jeffery Lyons guilty of first-degree murder of Malcolm O'Neil.

Anna shrieked for joy. "Justice!"

"Yes," Corpizio said. "And the Department of Justice has seized all the assets of Lyons's organization, the Endangered Earth Alliance."

"The effects of that man's greed will probably be felt for years to come."

"There'll be others like him," Corpizio said.

Anna's sense of relief remained undaunted.

"How are you doing?" he asked.

"A lot has changed." Anna said softly, "but at least now I can put the past behind me."

Now, from the scenic overlook, Anna drew in a deep breath of fresh air. She felt alive again as she climbed behind the wheel of her Jeep. At the valley bottom, Anna turned up the road toward the Fischer Creek Café and Gas Station where the local picnic was under way. Judging from the vehicles, the whole community turned out for the event. Anna felt honored to be among those invited.

She parked and wandered among the gingham-checked picnic tables, smoking barbecues, and children chasing balloons. Reuben was the first to spot her.

"My favorite fugitive has arrived!" he said. "Come meet my wife, Cassandra." Reuben craned his neck and searched the sea of heads. "My son, Cordell, is running around here somewhere."

Cassandra stepped forward and took Anna's hand in hers. "I'm so glad to finally meet you. If it wasn't for you standing up for my husband. Well, I never got a chance to properly thank you."

"It's not necessary." Anna smiled self-consciously and changed the subject. "So, what is this gathering all about?"

Suddenly, Grace Fischer appeared on the porch and rang the dinner triangle. "Can I have everyone's attention, please?"

The crowd congregated around the porch.

"Thank you all for coming." Grace dabbed at the corner of her eye with a tissue. "It's been a long time since we've gotten together."

Anna's gaze froze on the far side of the steps. There stood Lily Harrington. Lily, whose husband was killed by Milo Fischer! In her arms, a baby fussed and she tenderly kissed his tiny head of peach-fuzz hair. Lily looked up and smiled at Grace Fischer. Her face reflected nothing but good will and forgiveness.

"The barbecues are smoking and I don't want to keep everyone in suspense," Grace said. "So please welcome the new owners of the Fischer Creek Café and Gas Station!" Delighted chatter sprang from the cluster of neighbors as Grace called Dillon and his wife, Jody, to her side.

"It's true," Dillon said. "We worked out a purchase agreement and it's official. Don't worry, though. Mom doesn't plan on going into full retirement just yet."

"That's right," Jody cut in. "Grace has agreed to supply homemade pies and to divulge her closely guarded recipes—but only to me, of course." She giggled.

"Congratulations!" someone yelled, and others followed suit.

"We have so much to be grateful for," Grace said

as Charlie Waits stepped forward to say the blessing.

"Lord, thank you for great friends and for family." The pastor paused, looked at Peter with a father's pride, and continued. "And thank you for the restoration that only you can bring. In the precious name of Jesus, we ask that you bless the new owners of the Fischer Creek Café. Oh yeah, thank you for the fellowship here today and for the food we are about to eat. Amen."

"Let's celebrate," Dillon exclaimed and the party was under way.

Anna found it ironic that this family, who had been so deeply wounded by cultural warfare, would be the first to extend a healing hand. Across the picnic tables, environmentalists and ranchers spoke, finding common ground and forming bonds.

Someone offered a lemonade toast. "To new beginnings!"

Anna raised her glass. "New beginnings," she echoed.

HISTORIC NOTE

Although the gray wolf was reintroduced to the northern Rocky Mountains, including Yellowstone National Park and wilderness areas in Idaho, in 1995 and 1996, the controversy about wolves and the Endangered Species Act lives on today in both lore and current events. Wolf reintroduction has been a good news and bad news story. For radical environmentalists, the good news is that wolves have done very well; for ranchers and sportsmen, the bad news is that wolves have done very well.

The U.S. Fish & Wildlife Service under the Experimental Population provision of the Endangered Species Act carried out the reintroduction of wolves. As an experimental population, the U.S. Fish & Wildlife Service was able to issue a special rule that provided for more liberal take of wolves than would have otherwise been allowed had naturally occurring wolves been present in those areas. Mostly opposed in the West, the reintroduction planning process was very contentious, polarizing communities, threatening certain traditional economic activities and part of the western culture.

Prior to the reintroduction of the wolves, many people claimed that there were naturally occurring wolf populations within the ecosystems, and therefore, wolves should have been given full protection under the Endangered Species Act. Others frequently reported of wolves and wolf hybrids being illegally released into the mountainous areas near Yellowstone and in Idaho.

The reintroduced wolves, which were trapped in the Canadian Rockies where wolf populations thrive, did much better than anyone had predicted and by 2002 they met the recovery goals.

Soon after, the U.S. Fish & Wildlife Service began efforts to increase the level of State authority to manage the recovered population of wolves and the ground work was laid for their eventual removal from the Endangered Species List, a process called delisting. For several years there was contentious debate, mostly between the U.S. Fish & Wildlife Service and the State of Wyoming, concerning the adequacy of protection of a delisted population under the Wyoming Wolf Management Plan. Wyoming had proposed to classify the delisted wolves as a Predatory Animal in all of Wyoming except the wilderness areas adjacent to Yellowstone National Park. As a Predatory Animal, killing wolves would not have required a license, nor would their take be limited by any quota or bag limit. In a compromise effort to enable the U.S. Fish & Wildlife Service to proceed with the delisting effort, Wyoming expanded the area where licenses and limits would be required to include all of the viable wolf habitat in northwest Wyoming.

In February 2008, the U.S. Fish & Wildlife Service published a Final Rule delisting the Northern Rocky Mountain population of wolves. The Great Lakes population of wolves had already been delisted and the Southwest population would remain on the Endangered Species List.

On July 18, 2008, a Federal District Court Judge, in response to a lawsuit brought by environmentalists challenging the delisting decision, issued a preliminary injunction thus halting, as of this printing, the delisting of the Northern Rocky Mountain wolves and keeping the controversy alive in the hearts and minds of the people of the West and elsewhere.